A HARBOR OF RESENTMENT

DREW DUNMOORE

A HARBOR OF RESENTMENT

This book is dedicated to Henry. You always spoke the sweetest words, wore the fiercest sunglasses, and giggled the most with me in class when we were supposed to be paying attention. See you soon my friend…

"The Actors"

Celeste Ravenna - Raven haired beauty scarred by trauma

Detective Brian Bahn - Devilishly handsome leading man determined to help heal Celeste

Maybel Morgan - Feisty matriarch of Regal Palms and mother figure to Celeste

Jeffrey Morgan - Maybel's loving son and soon to be husband to Jill Jenson

Jill Jenson - Budding starlet and Jeffrey's fiancée

Jack Jenson - Business owner extraordinaire and full of more hot air than a balloon

Diane Deermark-Jenson - Former model and Jack Jenson's devoted wife

Leah Langley - Edgy jewelry designer and sexual competition to Jill Jenson

Vick Arnold - President of the Regal Palms Homeowners Association and Maybel's arch-nemesis

Kristen Campbell - Jill's lifelong BFF and rich California girl

Veronica Owens - Celeste's BFF and all-American beauty

Tom Fitzpatrick - Veronica's boyfriend and Regal Palms board member

Oscar Washington - Owner of the Velvet Sapphire and all-around cool guy

John Swormy - Jack's Head Machinist and lap dog

Chapter One

The Most Wonderful Time of the Year

When *she was a little girl, Celeste Ravenna thought boys were gross. They pushed and shoved, were loud, and worst of all, they spread cooties everywhere. Her first day attending kindergarten, the class bully tried stealing her wooden puzzle away from her. She held on to it for dear life, shouting at him and made sure she told the teacher what he did. Most days, the bully boy left her alone after that. Occasionally in the halls, he tried swatting at her, but she always ducked. When he pulled on her pigtails by the monkey bars, she gave him a swift playground kick to the shin running away immediately after. Celeste had been running from men ever since.*

Present day - December 2017

Detective Brian Bahn (pronounced BANE) entered stage left of Celeste's life when working some homicide cases at the building she lived in a few months earlier. Their paths not only crossed, but they amalgamated as peacefully as Pop Rocks in your mouth. Smooth with the ladies, rarely did Brian Bahn hear the word no. He glided through life with ease, and when troubles with women occurred, he just glided to the next one. He viewed each woman he got involved with as a beautiful gift for him to unwrap, but sometimes he got bored with his presents… and sometimes his presents divorced him, forcing him to pay alimony.

Most women found Brian to be like a wave in the ocean. They couldn't wait to surf, but Celeste held Brian at bay. If playing hard to get was what Celeste wanted, Brian knew he could play that game better than she. But what Brian failed to realize is that, for Celeste, it wasn't a game. It was *her* way of life. Celeste possessed a hard outer shell Brian hadn't been able to crack yet because in Celeste's past lived some deceptively addictive relationships that created an undercurrent of emotional scar tissue pulling her heart to the bottom of the ocean, and there it stayed like sunken treasure buried under the briny sand. Even though she kept her finances in perfect order, she never counted the cost of keeping her heart hidden. Heartbreak was her song, and independence and avoidance were the beats.

If given the opportunity, Brian would whisper sweet nothings in Celeste's ear to find out what lay beneath the surface. Brian spoke in a voice that affected Celeste greatly, and he was a force to be reckoned with. His deep voice sounded the way warm melted butter tasted, and when he called Celeste to ask her out, she couldn't say no. In fact, she could barely say anything at all. In mid-December, Brian and Celeste sailed onto the uncharted water of their first date. Brian asked Celeste if she wanted to pick a restaurant for dinner, and Celeste, never a woman to be indecisive, picked her favorite place.

Le Unione Ristorante was a little hole in the wall Italian place with cliché red and white checkered table clothes, artificial grape vines on the walls, and delicious cheesy breadsticks. When Brian picked her up, Celeste felt relieved he didn't have on his outdated sports coat. Instead, he wore jeans and a blue flannel shirt. Thank God he tucked it in, Celeste thought. Celeste topped her jeans off with a red V-neck sweater and paired them with black leather boots. Because Brian told her he had a surprise for her after dinner, she brought along a red and pink striped scarf in case it got cold. Her long dark hair hung loose that night. Her eyes were as black as coal but shined like diamonds. When she put on her war paint for the date, she chose a vivid shade of scarlet red to match her sweater. Celeste believed if you knew how to wear the right shade of red lipstick, you could use it as a weapon.

A pleasing smell of garlic invaded their nostrils at Le Unione Ristorante, where the friendly staff remembered Celeste. After the exotic Romanes hostess seated them in a secluded booth in the back, she looked at Brian, motioned to Celeste, and speaking in a heavy accent, she said, "You're a lucky man. So beautiful this one is."

Brian grinned like the Cheshire cat. "I am," he agreed.

Celeste opened her menu. "I don't know why I'm looking at the menu. I always order the same thing," she said, closing it.

"What are you going to have?"

"The Michael Angelo chicken—it's a chicken breast sauteed in a white wine sauce with onions, capers, mushrooms, olives, and peppers. It's my favorite." Celeste sipped from her water glass. She didn't want to admit it, but being around Brian made her nervous and her mouth dry like cotton.

"Oh, that sounds good," he said, perusing the menu. He closed it and looked at Celeste, holding his gaze on her for a while.

"What are you going to have?" Celeste asked, her mouth like a desert.

He winked and said, "I'm a simple man."

While they drank wine, broke bread, and waited for dinner, they discussed taboo topics like religion and politics. They were comfortable discussing these things with each other and found out they were both raised Catholic. They agreed the dogma of the religion didn't appeal to either of them, but the essence of spirituality stayed with them both. "There were just so many rules. I certainly couldn't live up to them," Celeste said with a laugh.

"Me either." Checking in on Celeste's emotional state, Brian asked, "How have you been doing since you came face to face with a murderer?"

The question jolted Celeste, and she held her breath for a few moments. She let out a long exhale.

Brain observed, "One breath says it all."

"I feel so foolish. I'm always so good at reading people, and I didn't realize… I mean… I guess I missed the signs…"

Brian reached out and touched her hand. "Better to be fooled than to be dead. Someone up above was looking out for you, kid."

Celeste nodded and pulled her hand away, grabbing for her glass of water. She felt the heat from him, and she wondered if she was like a moth to a flame or if she was the flame. She wanted to trust him and let her guard down, but she just couldn't do that yet. Baby steps, she told herself.

In a moment of honesty, Brian admitted to himself that Celeste made him feel like a schoolboy wondering if she liked him. He chased her. He tried to show his prowess by protecting her. He tried to lift her spirits by making her laugh, and he wanted to give his love away freely. He also wanted to push all her buttons just to get her to break and then soothe her.

Celeste, on the other hand, held onto her love tightly. She remembered that old saying: don't throw your pearls to the pigs. After two failed serious relationships, she placed her heart on ice. This did not easily deter Brian. He wanted to melt that hard frozen outer shell if it was the last thing he did.

"You know, I asked you out because your disfunction speaks to my disfunction," Brian said.

"Is it that obvious?"

"Well, keep in mind I am a world class detective."

"*World* class?" Celeste raised her eyebrows.

"Yeah, I've solved cases outside the U.S."

Celeste asked, "Where?"

"Mexico… Tijuana, to be precise. I solved the case of the missing cerveza." Brian smiled.

After he got Celeste to laugh, they talked about books and movies over dinner. *Ghost Busters* being at the top of Brian's list made Celeste wonder if a marshmallow fluff came after him, what would he do? She watched him twirl his spaghetti around his fork and shove meatballs into his mouth.

With dinner over, Brian wanted dessert, so they shared a piece of tiramisu. The espresso in it danced on their tastebuds and punched them with a zing of caffeine for the rest if the evening. He paid the bill and suggested they leave. After saying goodbye to the staff, a kiss on each cheek from the hostess sent Celeste on her way. The hostess kept her eyes on Brian and playfully waved goodbye to him.

Fortunately for Celeste's hair, Brian kept the top of his convertible up. "So, what's next? You said you had a surprise."

"I do. Have you ever been to Marvin's Gardens?" he asked, pulling out of the parking lot onto the road.

"I've heard of it, but I've never been there," Celeste answered, referring to the upscale nursery tucked away in a little coastal community.

He turned on his radio, which was set to the station playing Christmas music only. He sang, *"It's beginning to look a lot like Christmas!"*

Feeling embarrassed for him, Celeste hoped he would stop singing. Politely she said, "That sounds great." She wondered, was this tough guy into holiday fun?

In route to Marvin's Gardens, Brian asked Celeste about her work, and because she hated talking about her work, she gave a basic brief description of what all she did for a living.

After hearing the explanation of what being the supervisor of an insurance claims department entailed, he mused, "Sounds like a lot of pressure."

"It is. Sometimes I wish I could do something else for a living, but I don't know what else I could do and still earn as much money as I do now," Celeste said, feeling a little guilty. She never wanted to be ungrateful for her job, but as she aged, she felt her needs changing. "I'm good at what I do, but I sometimes feel unfulfilled by it. I think there must be more to life than processing insurance claims. However, I have a way of spotting the fraudulent claims from a mile away. My boss makes me double check everyone else's cases just in case they missed something. He says I'm the human lie detector. I've locked people down on a recorded line, making fraudulent claims more times than I can count. One of the most typical is a homeowner's DIY project goes wrong and they try to blame it on some sort of natural occurrence. I find it easy to sift the real claims from the false claims."

"We have that in common," he said, looking out his side mirror and changing lanes. "I can always tell when someone is lying, but I find what people don't say is just as important as what they do say."

Celeste knew this to be true. "Exactly… and there is one thing you can always ask that weeds out the liars."

"What's that?" Brian asked.

Celeste laughed and replied, "I can't tell you. It's my secret. If you ever make a false insurance claim, I'll need to weed you out."

"I have to admit when I first met you, I didn't think you liked me."

"I didn't. I'm sorry… I don't mean to be rude. I just thought you seemed arrogant and… kind of like an insensitive jerk."

"Ah, I get that a lot. In my line of work, I need to be decisive and confident. I can't show weakness," he explained.

Celeste thought of the famous quote and said it, "Every weakness contains within itself a strength."

"Are you saying I'm weak?"

Celeste laughed, shaking her head no. She shifted gears, and in a serious tone said, "I can't imagine how difficult your job must be." Until the horrible events that happened in her building recently (which you can read about in a book called *RENT TO KILL*), she'd never given much thought to what law enforcement really dealt with. She always thought it was just police dealing with traffic violations and drug busts. She now knew they deal with much more evil things… things she didn't want to think about and actively pushed out of her mind.

"It is difficult, and my work is never done, but every once in a while, I get to meet some pretty wonderful people." He looked over at her.

"You mean like Maybel?" Celeste asked, dodging a mushy moment, referring to her next-door neighbor, who Brian knew.

Brian laughed. "Yes, like Maybel."

Arriving at their destination, Brian parked and hopped out of the car, hurrying over to her door to open it, a sweet gesture in Celeste's mind. She got out and put on her scarf. It was 55°F that night, cold for California.

Walking along the sidewalk up to Marvin's Gardens, lights twinkled everywhere, and it looked like an enchanted Christmas forest wonderland. "This is so cool!" She looked around, taking it in.

"Yeah, I love this place," he said. He put his hand on the small of her back, guiding her over to the first shop. He hoped the smell of cinnamon would work like an aphrodisiac on her. Celeste wondered who else he brought to this place but wasn't about to ask him.

Entering the beautifully decorated Christmas shop felt like stepping into a winter paradise. Wreaths to bring joy to your front doors hung everywhere. Teardrop and icicle shaped ornaments dangled from pointy evergreen limbs, gleaming with gold and silver brilliance. Hand-blown glass lanterns from Europe popped with a shine like sparkling flutes of champagne. Little apricot toned balls with botanical designs nestled into miniature Christmas trees, glowing softly from the branches. Red and white peppermint twisties shimmered from their hooks. Black and red nutcrackers stood erect at attention, ready for duty. Baskets filled with handmade Schaller Santa's to adorn your home stood around just waiting to be purchased. Tabletop trees batched together in clusters of forest fun on huge oak display tables. The scent of warm cinnamon and cloves filled the air. Celeste breathed in deep, and a calm washed over her.

Brian smiled, knowing his surprise worked.

He held up two round red sparkly ornaments—one to each of his ears, playfully asking Celeste, "Do these earrings go with this outfit?" Then he set the ornaments down and put his head through the hole of a wreath, so it hung around his neck. "How about this necklace? Too much?"

"It makes your neck look skinny," Celeste said, giggling and examining a beautiful angel ornament with gold wings. She wondered what her Christmas tree would look like if she bought a whole host of them. A $30 price tag for one made her decide they were too rich for her blood.

An elegant-looking sales lady dressed in all black approached Brian. "Have you seen our Schallers this year? We had them custom designed by a European artist, and he used a special bronze sheen paint for Santa's bag of toys. Each one is hand painted."

Brian held it up and said to Celeste, "Look, Celeste! They hand painted Santa's sack!"

Celeste walked away giggling and checked out a basket of aquatic themed ornaments. She particularly liked the mermaids and gold starfish.

They poked around in other shops. The shopping temptation taunted Celeste at every turn, and she decided that before they left, she would buy a poinsettia plant as a Christmas gift for Maybel… and what the heck, she would buy herself one too. After browsing the stores, they headed back outside past the gift-wrapping station to the enchanting garden area, which had all the allure as the garden of Eden. When Brian reached for Celeste's hand to hold it, a flutter rippled through her.

Marvin's Gardens sold Christmas trees, fresh cut. She breathed in the crisp pine scent and breathed out the cold air. They walked along an evergreen lined path until they approached a quaint little coffee cart.

"Oh, we have to get a drink!" Brian said. The coffee stand sold a variety of holiday drinks and cookies. He studied the menu board, asking Celeste if she knew what she wanted.

"You go first," she said, still trying to decide.

"I'll have a mocha mint-chino with a caramel blast and a gingerbread twist," he said to the barista.

The young barista asked, "Would you like the butterscotch infused whipped cream on top?"

"Oh, yes, please!" Brian licked his lips. Celeste laughed, and he looked at her, asking what was so funny.

"That's a very elaborate drink order. I didn't think men ordered things like that."

"Delicious holiday beverages know no gender, Celeste."

"Here is your drink, sir." The barista merrily presented the beverage to him with a smile. A hard baked spicey gingerbread man cookie straddled the edge of the mug's rim, a cloud of butterscotch whipped cream floated gently on top of his minty mocha-chino, and a long candy cane swizzle stick poked out just waiting to stir it all up. "Would you like chocolate sprinkles, too?" the barista offered.

Brian's eyes lit up at the suggestion. "Please!"

Chocolate sprinkles cascaded down all over Brian's dollop of butterscotch whipped cream under the shaking hand of the barista. She asked Celeste, "What will you have?"

Celeste opted for her favorite holiday drink, answering, "A hot apple cider, please."

"Oh, classic—just like you!" Brian smiled.

Once they were both holding their warm beverages, they walked along until they came to a bench by a nativity scene. They nestled in under a bright bow shaped moon. Venus, looking like the brightest star of all, twinkled down on them from the east. Twinging and twanging harps and violins plucked the air and sprung out Christmas music joyfully in the background. The lyrics about a holy night brightened Celeste's mood, filling her heart with the mystery of a giving spirit and reminded her when light came into the world.

She turned her body towards Brian and looked at him. After dunking his gingerbread man into submission and drenching it in his dollop of whipped cream, he licked dripping cream off its leg. Celeste flinched and looked away, giving him a moment alone with it.

"Mmm," he moaned, "it's like a gingerbread delight!"

She turned back after he devoured it and asked, "When you were a child, what was your favorite Christmas present you ever got?" She sipped her cinnamon infused cider.

"Oh, man. That's a tough question. I got so many cool things as a kid, like remote control cars, Legos, a GI Joe doll, model airplanes. But I think the gift I used the most was my skateboard. I loved that thing and rode it all the time. I put stickers all over the bottom of it. I was fearless on it too. I thought I could jump over anything." Brian extended his arm on the back of the bench behind Celeste, leaning towards her a bit. "What was your favorite gift?"

"I think I'd have to say it was my baton. My dad gave it to me. I don't remember my dad being around much when I was a kid. He was always working and kind of emotionally distant to put it nicely… but I remember getting that baton like it was yesterday," Celeste answered.

"A baton? You mean like a nightstick?" he wondered.

Celeste laughed. "No! I mean like a twirling baton… you know… the kind the girls twirl around in parades," Celeste explained.

"Oh, yeah. Ok, I can picture you doing that. Did you wear a cute little outfit with a short skirt?" he asked.

"I was never in a parade. That was just an example. I just twirled it around in the backyard. I got pretty good at it… only hit myself on the top of my skull a few times. I still remember what it looked like. It was metallic candy apple red with white tips. I loved that thing!"

Brian laughed and asked, "Would just the tip hit your head? Or the whole thing?"

They reminisced about Christmas before heading out, making two stops on their way back to the parking lot. They did a whirl on the merry-go-round. Brian enjoyed watching Celeste straddle the horse, but when he did it, the molded metal saddle hit quite uncomfortably against his man parts. Wincing, he hung on tight as they bobbed up and down. Childhood memories danced through their minds as they sailed around and around.

They also stopped off at one of the stores so Celeste could purchase a couple of poinsettias. She bought an apple scented candle and elegant brass candle snuffer to go with it, a perfect gift for Maybel.

The December night air dropped colder, and Brian turned the heater on during the drive home, hoping to warm her up in more ways than one. Celeste left her scarf on and wished for some gloves. After a drive down the coast highway, Brian pulled up to her building. As usual, there were no parking spots on the street. Parking at Celeste's building was limited. "You can just drop me off in front of the building. You don't have to walk me back to my place. I know the parking here is difficult."

Brian, a bit disappointed, stopped his car in front of the building. Celeste took off her seatbelt and turned to look at him. "I had a really nice time tonight. Thank you for dinner," she said, moving a little closer to him.

Taking the cue, Brian looked deep into Celeste's eyes. He sheathed her lips with his kiss.

Celeste breathlessly noticed his kisses tasted like gingerbread. She hugged him and opened her door. "I need to get the poinsettias out of the back seat," she reminded him. She quickly grabbed her two plants, said goodbye, and closed the door with a bump of her hip. She hurried away towards her building. Unbeknownst to her, the angels kissed their date that night.

Driving away, Brian looked in his rearview mirror, noticing a smudge of red lipstick on his lips. If he didn't know better, he would have thought he just got punched in the mouth. It was going to be a fight for her heart, but Brian loved a good fight.

Chapter Two

Let's Dig Up the Past

January 2018, three weeks later

"**H**ave you been doing your affirmations?" Dr. Marilyn Fisher asked her patient.

"Yes, but I don't really believe them, and I feel strange saying them," Celeste replied, sitting on a comfortable couch in the dimly lit room of her therapist's office. Incense burned, and a waterfall trickled calmly in the corner. Zen music played softly in the background. None of this did anything to ease Celeste's anxiety.

"Well, that is kind of the point of them… to convince your mind," Dr. Fisher said, writing something on the notepad in front of her.

"The one I'm really having trouble with is 'I am safe in my home, and there is a divine power protecting me'." Celeste tried to shift her weight on the couch only to sink in further feeling like her rear end got trapped in quicksand.

"Let's explore that, Celeste," Dr. Fisher said, eager to help, "it's understandable why your mind would tell you that you aren't safe considering—"

"Considering a serial killer broke into my place and tried to kill me?" Celeste could hear and feel the hostile tone in her voice. She didn't mean to use that tone with her therapist, who she rather liked, but sometimes she couldn't help snapping.

"Yes… an unfortunate set of circumstances. However, he didn't physically harm you." Dr. Fisher looked at Celeste, waiting for her to respond.

"That's true… at least not physically," Celeste said. She couldn't bring herself to discuss the psychological harm the killer inflicted on her.

"You can also rest assured knowing he is in jail," Dr. Fisher added.

"In Jail but not prison," Celeste pointed out, feeling the need to argue with her therapist because the statement Dr. Fisher made seemed naïve to Celeste.

"You'll be testifying against him, and with all the evidence you said your boyfriend has against him, he should be in prison soon," Dr. Fisher replied.

"He's not my boyfriend," Celeste said.

"Ok… maybe not, but Brian seems to care for you, and you said you went on a very nice date with him," Dr. Fisher prodded, referencing Celeste's evening with Detective Bahn. "Every cloud has a silver lining. There may have been horrific events that took place in your condo complex, but on the positive side, you met someone who really seems to understand how rare you are."

Celeste dismissively said, "It was just one date. Besides, he said he asked me out because he thinks I'm as dysfunctional as he is."

Dr. Fisher understood Celeste was not an open book. The previous sessions with her patient made that clear. Detective Brian Bahn referred Celeste to Dr. Fisher. She and Brian both knew Celeste was experiencing post-traumatic stress because of some abominable events that took place at the building she lived in. Brian thought Dr. Fisher could help Celeste process the horrific events she went through recently. "Well, maybe you two can put the fun in dysfunctional. You said you had a good time. Are you planning to go on a second date with him?"

The question made Celeste feel silly, like she was in high school again, and one of her friends was asking her if she liked a boy. "Maybe if he asks me out again."

"You could always ask him out," Dr. Fisher suggested.

"No."

"Why wouldn't you ask him out?" Dr. Fisher wondered.

"I'm not sure how serious I want things to get, and I don't want to mislead him. I'm very comfortable on my own. Plus, we're both very busy. He works a lot of over-time, and I'm trying to sell my place. I really need to focus on that," Celeste explained. Back in the summer of 2017, she met Brian when he was working on a case at Regal Palms, the building she lived in. He was in his 40s like her but twice divorced, unlike her. Feeling quite fond of Celeste, he asked her out when the case was over.

"You know, if you isolate yourself when you're feeling overwhelmed, you probably had to solve a lot of problems on your own as a kid."

"I try to never rely on anyone for anything. My dad never really helped with anything. The few times I tried to go to him with something, he just made things worse. He was very self-absorbed, almost narcissistic. I think we discussed this be-fore," Celeste said.

"Yes, we did. An abusive parent who inflicts psychologi-cal and emotional abuse on a child creates psychological war-fare within the family, and because these children grow up on emotional battlefields, they become adults who are still stuck in fight-or-flight mode. You're an insightful person, Celeste. I know you will be able to shift your energy."

"No one will ever know the abuse it took to become this insightful. I think some people are just meant to suffer. I mean, if I end the battle, I'd have to let go of all this long-suffering stuff I do." A bitter laugh escaped Celeste, and she added, "I can't stay at my place. I need to leave."

"So, you've made up your mind to move?" Dr. Fisher asked.

Celeste let out a deep breath.

"Celeste," Dr. Fisher's aged face was serious, and she went on, "I really think you're trying to run away from your problems. When your own mind torments you, you need to remember those thoughts and emotions are only visiting. Don't invite them to stay. The mind can take you to some beautiful places if you let it, and Brian could help bring healing to your life."

"It's not just about fear or avoidance. The building really isn't practical. It's far from my work, takes forever to get through the parking lot and up the elevator, and I can't even have a washer and dryer hook up in my place. I've built up some equity and can afford something better now," Celeste said.

"Those all sound like good reasons, but won't you miss Maybel? I know she's like a mother to you," Dr. Fisher asked, referring to Celeste's next-door neighbor.

"We will keep in touch. When all that craziness was going on, her son Jeffrey bought her an iPhone. We can Facetime. Also, she can Uber over to my place for our Saturday lunches, and she might not stay in the building either. Her son wants her to move to a retirement home. Because of everything that happened at Regal Palms over the summer and fall, he doesn't think it's safe for her to stay."

Dr. Fisher could sense that Celeste's mind was made up. She decided to discuss another topic they touched on during their last therapy session. "Have you had your reoccurring nightmare lately?"

"Once… around the end of last month," Celeste answered. The reoccurring stress dream they were talking about was one in which Celeste gets trapped in a bus that goes over a cliff, landing in the ocean, thrusting her face to face with a deadly shark.

"Have you figured out what it means?" Dr. Fisher adjusted the chunky beaded bracelet around her wrist and stared at Celeste, waiting for an answer.

"No, I thought that was what I was paying you for," Celeste replied.

Dr. Fisher chuckled. "It means more if you figure it out for yourself."

"Well, like I said, I saw *Jaws* when I was a young child, and it traumatized me. I never wanted to go into the ocean after that. I was even afraid to take a bath, and I was convinced he lurked under my bed and in my closet. Do you have any thoughts about what the dream could mean?"

"I do," Dr. Fisher answered, smiling as she pushed her gold-rimmed glasses further up on her nose. An older woman in her 60s, Dr. Fisher remained attractive by dying her hair a vivid shade of strawberry blonde. That day, as she counseled Celeste, she wore a long bohemian style skirt and black turtle-neck. Her clothes fit her soothing aura.

Celeste asked, "Are you going to tell me what you think it means? Or does that cost extra?"

"I think it's about love. You mentioned when you get really stressed at work, you have the dream, but I don't think it has anything to do with work. At work you are very confident and capable, and you are the shark… but in love, you feel like the prey. You don't like being hunted. It makes you feel vulnerable, and you most definitely don't like feeling vulnerable," Dr. Fisher explained.

Celeste was unsure how she felt about what she just heard. She frowned and looked down at her hands. She fought back tears from the sting of the nerve Dr. Fisher hit.

Dr. Fisher handed her a Kleenex. "Celeste, the stakes are high. It's OK to be vulnerable, but it's not OK to let a chance at love pass you by."

"It's not OK to be vulnerable. That's how you get hurt," Celeste said.

"It's part of life," Dr. Fisher said gently.

"I've already been vulnerable in my past, and it got me nowhere. It was painful and made it difficult to focus on my work. I don't have the energy for all of that now. My career is too important," Celeste reasoned again.

"Humans are emotional by nature. Emotion is a gift, but if we are too strongly driven by emotion, it can be very misleading," Dr. Fisher said.

"I agree. We can think we care about someone when we really don't," Celeste said.

"No, that's not what I mean. Your fear of being vulnerable and getting hurt is driving you to be very closed off from love," Dr. Fisher explained.

"So," Celeste said defensively.

"So, love is God's greatest gift to us. I would encourage you to let go of your fear and receive the gift," Dr. Fisher replied.

Celeste sighed and nodded.

"Let's stop here. This is a good place to pause," Dr. Fisher said, smiling at her patient. "I want to leave you with a homework assignment. This week, try consciously acting out of love and not fear, and remember, Brian is not an enemy you have to battle. He's an ally."

"OK, I'll try," Celeste said half-heartedly. She and Dr. Fisher set their next appointment. Celeste said goodbye and exited the office, feeling relieved the appointment was over. Brian suggested she go to Dr. Fisher to help with the PTSD, and when she agreed, she didn't realize how much other junk the appointments would bring up.

Walking through the parking lot, she held back tears. Once in her car, she let herself cry. She hated how foolish she'd been trusting someone who was a killer. She hated that years ago she let herself get involved with a man who cheated on her. She hated she still had life dreams she hadn't achieved yet. And most of all, she hated how much the grief for her deceased mother and father hurt. She was tired of visiting these places in her sessions with Dr. Fisher. She wondered how long PTSD would last. She blew her nose and took a few deep breaths before driving home.

Celeste pulled into her designated parking spot in her building's underground parking structure and took the elevator up to the ninth floor. She thought again about what a pain it was to always wait for the elevator, and it smelled faintly of stale cigarette smoke. Once inside her place, she flipped on the lights and saw her poinsettia still sitting on the counter. A few dead pedals laid curled up on the bar counter, and more pedals still on the plant had turned brown. Next to the plant sat a long rectangular gold box, the kind the florist puts long stem roses in. In it rested the gift Brian had left on her doorstep the day after Christmas. When she peeked into the box, the tissue paper crinkled as she pulled it back, and she found a shiny red baton nestled in the box. That made her smile.

The card attached read:

"Celeste,

Sorry your Christmas gift is late. I had to work a double homicide on Christmas day and couldn't get away. Try not to hit yourself on the head with this.

Brian"

It was not the most romantic note she'd ever been given, but it made her laugh. Receiving the gift made her feel a little guilty she didn't get him anything.

Celeste set her purse down next to the gold box and the plant and walked into the kitchen. She wanted to stretch out the last remnants of Christmas, so she got out a decorative bowl with pinecones and pine branches etched into it. She filled it with water and clipped off the two poinsettia blooms that were still alive. She floated the vibrant red blooms in the water so she could see them in a new way. She set the bowl on her bar counter next to a votive candle, lit the candle, and as she stared into the flame, tranquility washed over her. She turned on some classical music to help relax.

Her little bird, Birino, flew down from his perch on her bookcase and landed on her bar countertop. He walked along it towards her, as if to greet her. She smiled at him. He hopped up onto the edge of the decorative bowl. He fluttered his wings and jumped into the water. He splashed around a bit. Apparently, he thought it was his own personal bird bath. Celeste laughed at him and headed back to her kitchen.

She took out some salmon from her freezer for dinner and a knock hit her front door. Looking through the peek hole revealed the top of her neighbor Maybel's silver-haired head. Celeste greeted her 79-year-old friend with a smile.

"Hello dear, how are you? How was your session today?" Maybel inquired. Maybel lived in the building since 1958 when it was built. For Maybel, even though time passed, not much changed for her. She still believed you should lend your neighbor a cup of sugar and expect nothing in return. She was from a simpler time when, on Friday nights, you piled the kids and blankets into the station wagon and headed out to the drive-in. Saturdays were for popping Jiffy Pop and watching Dick Clark. She didn't understand why everyone always had their faces buried in their cell phones now.

"She gave me a homework assignment," Celeste responded.

Maybel encouraged her, "Well, you're a bright girl. I'm sure it will be easy for you."

Celeste was going to tell herself to forget to do it. "What's new with you?" Celeste asked.

Maybel said excitedly, "I have big news! Jeffrey and Jill got engaged! They are going to get married in April!" Maybel put her hands over her heart.

Celeste only met Jill once at the last year's Halloween party held on the roof of their building. Jeffrey, Maybel's son, dressed as a monk, and Jill wore a nun's costume–long habit, short skirt. "They are going to break their vow of celibacy?" Celeste asked.

"Apparently so, and Jeffrey said Jill's parents will be paying for the wedding. Jill wants to get married on a boat. With my fixed income, I'm a little relieved I don't have to foot the bill. I am going to have a small engagement dinner at my place for them. You're invited." Maybel smiled at Celeste. After Maybel's husband George passed away, feeling much sympathy for her, Celeste befriended Maybel. Celeste became like the daughter Maybel never had, and since Celeste lost her mother at a young age, Maybel's care for her felt quite comforting.

"OK, just let me know when," Celeste said.

Maybel imagined herself as cupid in this scenario and said, "Next Thursday at 6 PM. I invited Brian too. Hope you don't mind."

Celeste paused because she hadn't seen Brian since their date in December. He'd left her the gift the day after Christmas, and she texted him to say thank you. Other than that, they hadn't communicated for several weeks. She felt awkward. "OK," she consented.

"Great! I'll be making my homemade lasagna. It's one of Jeffrey's favorites. I've also invited Jill's parents and Jill's maid of honor. Her other bridesmaid can't make it." Maybel was one of the best cooks Celeste knew. She'd eaten Maybel's lasagna before, and it was nothing short of legendary.

"Do you want me to bring anything?" Celeste offered.

"No, just Brian," Maybel said.

"Alright, I got it," Celeste said, taking the hint. She and Maybel chatted a while longer before Maybel went back to her place.

Once alone, Celeste texted Brian: **Maybel just let me know she invited you and me to Jeffrey and Jill's engagement dinner next week.**

She went back into her kitchen and made dinner. As she sat down on the couch ready to eat, she heard her phone bing. Brian texted back: **I'll be there with bells on! Looking forward to seeing you again.**

Celeste texted back: **After all the Christmas decorations you tried on at Marvin's Gardens, I'm not sure if you are speaking literally or figuratively, but see you next week!**

Chapter Three

Always a Bridesmaid Never a Bride

Maybel cooked for two days prior to the engagement dinner. The lasagna, an old family recipe, called for scratch-made meatballs and sauce. To put it together, she strewed cooked noodles all over her tidy kitchen. When she assembled all the ingredients, chunks of meatballs were nestled into creamy heavenly clouds of seasoned ricotta cheese and topped with the sweet and spicey marinara sauce filled with secret ingredients. A labor of love this was for her son Jeffrey, and Maybel loved her forty-two-year-old son Jeffrey to no end.

The day of the engagement dinner, Maybel cleaned her place from top to bottom. She carefully set the table, a small square Formica table that could seat up to eight, if everyone squeezed together. The guest list included her son Jeffrey, his new fiancé Jill, Jill's parents Jack and Diane, Jill's friend Leah, Celeste, and Brian. Maybel met Jill a few times and did not know her very well. She hoped to get to know her better. Being protective of her son, she hoped Jill was good enough for him. Maybel had Jeffrey a bit late in life. She and George tried for so long that they finally gave up. Then, at 37, she got pregnant with her only son, and he meant the world to her.

Brian stopped at Celeste's place to pick her up for the dinner. Celeste, wearing a razor back electric blue dress she wore to work with a blazer, now stood at her front door without the blazer on. Brian wore his outdated sports coat and Celeste wondered if it had shoulder pads in it… or were those his shoulders.

"You look nice!" he said, heading around the corner to Maybel's condo.

"Come in, come in, you two! You are the first ones here. Would you like some wine?" Maybel offered them "Two Buck Chuck". Dean Martin sang "That's Amore" softly in the background from her record player. Maybel couldn't think of any music more romantic than him.

With wine in hand, Brian and Celeste sat down on the couch in Maybel's small living room, looking out at the view of the north side of Sunshine Beach. Brian rested his arm along the back of the couch behind Celeste. Celeste stiffened a bit. Maybel, making a mental note of it, lovingly set out the charcuterie board right before a knock at the door. She went to answer it, and Brian grabbed a piece of salami getting greasy fingers. Celeste heard several voices at the door, one of which she knew belonged to Jeffrey. This made her smile. Brian kept snacking, and Celeste whispered to him, "You dropped an olive on the floor."

A few moments later, Jeffrey, Jill, Jack, Diane and Leah appeared in the living room. Maybel did all the introductions and Brian stood up to shake Jeffrey's hand. "Congratulations! I heard you two are leaving the monastery."

Jeffrey chuckled a nice belly laugh, and his handsome face framed by his clean-cut hair beamed. "Yeah, we're breaking our vows to make a new vow! I almost didn't recognize you without your green paint face," Jeffrey said to Brian.

Celeste stood to greet everyone and shake hands. "Congratulations and welcome to the family," she said to Jill, hugging her. Because of Maybel's hospitality, Celeste also felt like they were family.

Jill resembled a beautiful blond starlet destined for Hollywood, but for now, working under the umbrella of her daddy's company would have to do. Her coy caramel-colored eyes melted Jeffrey's heart. Her pouty pink bunny lips gave him sweet kisses, and her tiny little button nose crinkled whenever he did something she disapproved of, which was often. Her petite figure and sun-drenched skin gave her the appearance of a perfect little California angel with her perfect California education. Her taste was expensive, and Jeffrey still had no idea how he was going to keep up with it.

"Oh, thank you! We are so excited! We've decided to get married on a *boat*. It sails around the harbor the whole time," Jill said, bubbling over. "What is that noise?" She crinkled her nose and her haughty eyes looked around Maybel's condo.

"Well, it's Dean Martin, dear," Maybel explained, pointing to her record player.

"I haven't seen one of those in years," Jill's mother said, frowning at the turntable.

Jill bent down to look at the appetizers and said, "Oh, look at this charcuterie board. How nice… I guess I can have an olive or two if they didn't touch anything else."

"Jill is vegan now," Jeffrey explained to his mother, grabbing a fistful of Fontina cheese wrapped in prosciutto. Jeffrey, being of average height and muscular, wore cargo shorts, a t-shirt, and flip-flops that day, knowing he could always be comfortable at his mom's house. He worked long hours fighting fires for the city of Malmark.

"Vegan? What is that?" Maybel asked.

"I don't eat any meat or any animal products," Jill explained.

Maybel's brow furrowed. "Oh."

Oh boy, Celeste thought, knowing Maybel's lasagna contained meat lots of meat: ground beef, Italian sausage, ground pork. She changed the subject, asking, "And you must be Leah?" Celeste looked at Jill's friend and extended her hand.

"Yes, I'm the maid of honor and Jill's business partner. Nice to meet you." Leah held out a skinny hand attached to a long, bronzed arm. Leah didn't like for people to know this, but she lived in the valley before moving closer to the beach. Never having enough money, she hustled to keep up. She also strived for her looks to be on point. She bleached her long teeth that poked out of her mouth, threaded her thick eyebrows, and waxed every which way. Her icy blue eyes drooped just a little, especially when a man broke her heart. A thin gold lip ring encircled her plump bottom lip, and another piercing penetrated her tongue. A beautiful hand beaded coral necklace dangled and bounced around between her bosoms. Leah may not have come from money like Jill did, but she could out-design Jill any day of the week, and they both knew it.

"Nice to meet you too, and this is Brian," Celeste said, turning her body towards Brian.

Leah turned her tanned slender figure towards Brian and shook his big, firm hand. She flipped her long chestnut-colored extensions back, so they caressed her pokey shoulders. She tilted her head, batting her eyelashes faster than a hummingbird's wings while sucking the sugar water out of a bird feeder. "So nice to meet you, Brian," she neighed like a horsey ready to ride. Leah was a smart little filly and knew exactly what track she wanted to run. "What do you do for a living, Brian?"

Brian shook her hand and wondered if she had anything else pierced. "I'm a detective for the city of Sunshine Beach."

"Oh, how exciting! I bet you've seen a lot of action," Leah said, raising her eyebrows at him.

She is flirting with him right in front of me, Celeste thought. She looked at Brian, who grinned from ear to ear while Leah still held his hand. Brian always derived a lot of pleasure from evoking that reaction from women, especially women as sultry as Leah. He looked her up and down.

"Well, everyone, dinner is all ready to go. We can sit down now," Maybel announced. She instructed everyone where their place at the table was. Leah tried to take the chair next to Brian, but Maybel steered her away. "No dear, your seat is over here by me," she said, gently grabbing her arm leading her away. Maybel and Leah sat at the head of the table side by side with Celeste and Brian at the opposite end of the table, side by side. Jeffrey and Jill sat on the side of the table that had their backs to the window, and Jill's parents, Jack and Diane, sat on the opposite of Jeffrey and Jill with their view to the north of the city. The bubbling pan of lasagna rested in the middle of the table on two hot pads—a nice cheesy crust baked on the top of it! A bountiful bowl of fresh salad sat on one side of the lasagna, and a basket of hot baked bread sat on the other side. Two bottles of chianti breathed at each end of the table. After Maybel said grace, Jeffrey dished up the lasagna for everyone.

Jill informed Maybel she didn't say grace because she's Buddhist.

"Oh, this is my favorite! Thanks Mom!" Jeffrey said, excitedly excavating a spatula full of lasagna from the pan. When a glorious cheese pull stretched from the pan, Jeffrey was oblivious to the disgusted look on Jill's face.

"Jill, there is meat in the lasagna. I didn't know you were vegetarian now, but there is salad and bread and olives and wine," Maybel offered, trying to be a gracious hostess.

"She's not vegetarian. She's *vegan*," Diane corrected. She was a proud, stuffy lady, who wore her hair long back in the day when she modeled, but now kept it on a short leash. A string of pearls the oysters sacrificed for her adorned her regal neck. Her conservative camel-colored sweater set denied her of any flashy attention now. A woman who gave up much for her husband's success, she was.

Maybel stopped pursing her lips to drink more wine.

"Well, I'm not either, so I'm going to dig in!" Brian put an enormous piece of lasagna in his mouth. He ate with gusto and so did Jeffrey—almost like they were racing each other to see who could finish first.

After the salad and bread were passed around, Maybel held up her wineglass to make a toast. With Chianti in the air, she said, "To Jeffrey and Jill, may they live happily ever after!" Maybel chugged her glass of wine and swiftly poured herself another.

Jack held up his glass and clinked it to Jeffrey's. His voice boomed, "We're excited to have you be part of our family, son. We can't wait for you to join the family business, too." Jack and Diane built an empire for themselves, and Jack loved to look down at his loyal subjects. He filled up his plate, not afraid to bite off more than he could chew. His expensive blue blazer smelled faintly of ocean air from a day on the yacht. Jack possessed an insatiable appetite for many things. No matter how much money he earned, it could never keep up with how much money he could spend. Whenever he signed a new deal, he salivated over it like a dog with a scrap of beef. His other appetite in the bedroom Diane had long since given up on trying to satisfy.

Celeste swore she saw Maybel bristle at Jack's comment. She also observed Leah dripping a little sauce on her chin. Leah caught Brian's eye, wiped off the sauce, and put her twig finger in her mouth to lick it off.

Brian went back in for seconds of lasagna. "Maybel, you really outdid yourself. This is the best lasagna I've ever had!" Brain moaned in delight with a mouth full of homemade goodness.

Celeste noticed Diane barely ate. Like mother, like daughter, she thought. "Jill, tell us more about your wedding plans," Celeste prompted, trying to make conversation.

Jill perked up, put her fork down, and spoke, "Oh yeah! So, we rented a lovely multi-level boat called The Knot Your Nuptials, and…," she went on twirling her finger in circles saying, "it sets sail around the harbor while we get married. We'll say our vows on the main deck at sunset. After that, we go into the enclosed part of the main deck, where we all have drinks and dinner. Then, we tiptoe up to the third level of the boat where Jeff gets to playfully smear just a touch of frosting on my nose, and then the cake will be served. After that, we dance the night away! The boat has a level below the main deck, but I don't want anyone going down there except to go to the bathroom. I mean, *below deck*—that just sounds so gross. I decided on my colors for the wedding: aqua blue, teal, purple, and forest green, like the colors on peacock feathers!" Jill clapped her hands, letting out a squeal of delight. "My wedding is going to be amazing!"

"That sounds lovely," Celeste said, noticing Leah was now staring seductively at Jeffrey. This woman was like a little piranha, Celeste thought.

"Yeah, and I'm going to ask all the guests to wear only those colors as well! It's going to be so wonderful!" Jill exclaimed. "Also, I was asked to do a spread in a popular woman's bridal magazine! It's just a magazine article, but hopefully it will lead to commercials and commercials will lead to some bigger acting roles. I keep telling Daddy we need to film some commercials for the business so that I can star in them."

Leah asked, "What magazine are you going to be in? No offense, Jill, but you're not really tall enough to be a model. Normally models are my height and photogenic like me."

Jill snapped back, "Well, Leah, I think the whole point of the shoot is to photograph someone who has actually been proposed to. That's why they asked me and not you."

Celeste could have sworn she saw steam come out of Leah's ears.

"What about your wedding shower?" Maybel asked, "Will Leah be throwing it?"

"I've been so busy with our jewelry business that I won't have time," Leah said, sipping her third glass of wine. "Jill understands, don't you, Jill?" Leah asked in a cool tone.

Jill nodded.

Celeste sensed some sort of unspoken agreement between Jill and Leah.

Jill cleared her throat, mustered up some courage and shot back, "Besides, with the tight budget Leah is always on, she'd never be able to afford to throw me a nice shower."

Celeste noticed Leah's warm olive colored skin turned a deep shade of raspberry, as she burned from Jill's remark.

Leah smirked. "Well, we know you certainly can't pay for your own shower, since your credit cards are maxed out."

A bristle performed a duet off Jack and Diane, ricocheting between the two of them with an embarrassed rhythm.

Celeste noticed Jill's beachy golden skin turned the color of a pink rose as she fumed from Leah's remark. She wondered why these two were friends.

"OK, then, I would be more than happy to throw you a wedding shower!" Maybel said to Jill.

Jill smiled politely and looked reluctant. "I guess that would be ok. Mom, are you ok with that?" Jill asked. Diane nodded her perfectly sophisticated head. Diane certainly didn't want to host the shower herself. All those ridiculous wedding shower games were beneath her.

"Well, then that's settled! Celeste, would you like to help me plan it?" Maybel asked, putting Celeste on the spot.

Celeste wanted to say no. "Well, I'm putting my condo on the market next week, so I might be kind of busy with that—"

Surprised, Brian asked, "You're selling your place?"

"Yeah, I told you that before, remember?"

"Yeah, I remember, but I thought maybe you changed your mind," he replied.

Celeste shook her head.

"Oh! I'd love to check out your place sometime! This building is so cool! It's like from the 60s or something. I've been wanting to move out of my apartment *foreeeeever*." Leah said, singing the word forever and feeling her wine.

"Sure, I'll keep you posted," Celeste replied.

"Well, either way, I'm happy to plan the shower. So, who's ready for some spumoni ice cream?" Maybel offered.

"Oh, I don't eat gluten or dairy," Jill said.

A priceless look cashed in on Maybel's face and she let out a sigh. "I have some fruit. Would you like a banana, dear?"

Celeste suppressed a giggle. Jeffrey, Brian, and Jack all took two scoops each. Wedding and shower plans were discussed before the night ended. Celeste and Brian left first. Brian wanted to make sure he walked her back to her door. He knew they had the killer in jail, but he still felt compelled to protect her.

"Why did that dinner feel so awkward?" Brian asked Celeste when they reached her door.

Celeste laughed and shook her head. "It was like an episode of *The Real Housewives*."

"A what?"

"Never mind. Jill and Leah act like they don't even like each other, and maybe also because Maybel is having a hard time letting go of her only child."

"Jeff is hardly a child. He's in his 40s. Maybe Jill and Leah could mud wrestle to settle their animosity towards each other," Brian said, and laughed.

Celeste frowned at him.

He went on, "It doesn't have to be mud. It could be Jell-O, or sugar free Jell-O if they are watching their carbs."

Celeste continued to frown. "That is so sexist!"

Brian loved eliciting this reaction from her. He continued to laugh, asking, "Did you see the way Leah flirted with Jeff? And right in front of Jill."

"Yeah, and I saw the way she flirted with you, too." Celeste looked up at Brian and smiled.

Brian grinned. "Well, that's to be expected. Women can't resist my sexy sexual sex appeal."

Celeste impulsively reached up, cupped his face with her hands, and kissed him passionately. Seeing another woman flirt with him made her realize she cared about him. His hands roamed around on her pear-shaped hips and their lips got friendly with each other.

"Will you be my date for their wedding?" he asked. Brian still wanted to have a dance with her since he missed the opportunity at the Halloween party.

"Yes. Do you have a peacock-colored shirt?" she asked.

"I'll have to buy one," he answered. "I'll be counting the days until I can strut my feathers in front of you," he said, and winked. They parted ways after another sweet goodnight kiss.

He's not your enemy, Celeste reminded herself, locking her front door. She stripped off her electric blue dress and took a cold shower.

Chapter Four

Love Squared

In the days to follow the engagement dinner, Celeste continued to prepare her condo to be listed on the market. Her savvy realtor, Traci, helped her look around for a new place closer to Celeste's work. Traci planned for an open house for Celeste's condo on Sunday, the day after Jill's wedding shower. Celeste kept busy cleaning her condo, pre-packing, and looking online at new places.

Maybel kept busy organizing the wedding shower for Jill. As usual, she went over to Celeste's place around noon for their weekly Saturday lunch. Celeste prepared spinach salads for them, topped off with bacon, hard-boiled eggs, and mushrooms. She waited until Maybel got to her place before pouring the warm vinaigrette dressing on it.

"The engagement dinner was really nice," Celeste said, sipping her peach iced tea.

"Thank you, dear. You know, I feel bad for saying this, but I don't really like Jill." Maybel put her napkin on her lap.

"I don't want to upset you by asking this, but do you think it could be because you… maybe feel like you're losing Jeffrey?" Celeste took a bite of her wilted salad.

Maybel shook her head and answered, "Something is off with her."

"Maybe it's because she's vegan and wouldn't eat your lasagna." Celeste smiled.

Maybel shook her head. "Oh, don't get me started on that! Two days I spent making the lasagna for them, and Jeffrey didn't even mention ahead of time she doesn't eat meat. I mean, I could have made pasta fagioli for her if I had known."

"She doesn't eat gluten either," Celeste reminded Maybel.

"What?" Maybel asked.

"Never mind."

"I also get the sense he doesn't know her very well. I think they're rushing into this too fast. I mean, I know she's a pretty gal, so I see what he likes about her, but they are quite different. She's a lot younger than him, too."

"Opposites attract," Celeste said.

"I just hope he's making the right decision. You know he also dated Leah," Maybel said.

"Are we sure Leah is over Jeff? She flirted with him the whole night. Even Brian noticed."

"I thought Leah was going to try to sit on Brian's lap at dinner!" Maybel laughed and went on, "Maybe I should set Leah up with Vick."

"Vick?" Celeste wondered. Vick held the position of homeowners' association board president at Regal Palms and kept a long-standing rivalry brewing strong with Maybel over who is/was the better HOA president.

"Dear, I don't mean to pry, but I noticed how stiff you are with Brian. A man like that will not wait forever, and with women like Leah throwing themselves at him, he might not be able to resist temptation," Maybel warned.

"I don't think a man like Brian ever resists temptation," Celeste replied, remembering how the waitress at El Unione reacted to him… and even the barista at Marvin's Garden's, who so obviously blushed when Brian smiled and winked at her.

"I know Vick is not the most handsome man around, but he is freakishly tall, and women like that. Maybe he could help divert Leah's attention away from Brian. I think Vick is fully recovered from the attack." Whispering, Maybel said, "You know, someone rumored that his man parts got crushed during the attack last summer."

"Oh, how awful. Who told you that?" Celeste asked.

"Don't worry about that, dear. The point is, he is doing much better now," Maybel said sympathetically.

"Would you like some coffee?" Celeste offered.

"Have I ever turned down a cup?"

While Celeste got them coffee and coconut macaroons for dessert, she asked Maybel to update her on everything she planned for Jill's wedding shower. Celeste found out the date had been set, the Rec room at Regal Palms reserved, invitations mailed out, peacock colored table clothes and decorations purchased, and Jill's mom Diane offered to pay for a caterer for the shower. They were using a company that does vegan food. Maybel thought it was sweet of Diane to offer, but really, Diane feared Maybel would cook food too heavy for a spring bridal shower.

"The entire menu for the shower will be vegan?" Celeste sipped her coffee.

"Yes. She decided on some sort of chickpea salad, cauliflower crust pizza with roasted red peppers and miniature gluten-free strawberry tarts," Maybel answered.

"Pizza? But I don't think vegans eat cheese."

"Oh, they put some sort of fake cheese on it. I'm going to make sure I eat before the shower, so I don't get hungry," Maybel said. "I offered to make food for the shower. I've got some great party recipes in my Betty Crocker cookbook like ham and cheese puffs, stuffed mushrooms, and Swedish meatballs, but Jill insisted all the food must be vegan. If you ask me, I think that's kind of selfish of her."

"I think the food sounds delicious. Have you decided on any games for the shower?" Celeste asked, dreading the idea of having to play them.

"Yes, two games. We will play the one where you break into groups and use toilet paper to make a wedding dress, and the other game is the one where everyone gets a plastic ring at the beginning of the shower. Then, anytime you hear someone say 'bride' or 'wedding', you can take away their ring. The person with the most rings at the end gets a prize," Maybel said. She purchased two bottles of fruity sparkling Italian wine for the prizes.

"With the wedding getting so close, is Jill getting stressed out? Does she have her dress?" Celeste asked.

"It sounds to me like her and her mother have things under control. The wedding invitations have gone out. She bought a lovely designer dress. They rented the boat, and they're using a caterer the boat company recommended, and the cakes will be from a local bakery here in Sunshine Beach," Maybel said.

"Is all the food at the wedding going to be vegan?" Celeste asked.

"No, Jill's mother talked her into doing a normal buffet with beef, chicken, and salmon, but there will be one or two vegan options served. I guess because of their family business, they invited a lot of clients, and Jill's mother said they needed to make sure they served traditional food. There will also be a full *open* bar."

For the first time, it occurred to Celeste she would have to go on a boat on the ocean. She felt a twinge of anxiety. Her deeply rooted phobia of sharks circled around her mind. She felt relieved booze would be served. She punched the thought of being on the ocean out of her mind. "So, what was all that talk about when Jack said he was excited Jeff was going to join their family business?"

With sadness, Maybel said, "I'm not sure. I asked Jeffrey about it. He said their business is some sort of plastic molds, metal molds, jewelry making and things like that. Jack offered Jeffrey a job, and he is considering leaving the fire department to work for them. I don't think it's a good idea, but it's his life."

"And Jill and Leah have a business together?" Celeste asked.

"Yes, it's under the umbrella of Jill's dad's business, some sort of jewelry design business. I think Leah does most of the designs, Jill does sales, and her family's business manufactures the jewelry. They work out of Jack's warehouse down by the docks near the harbor." Maybel took a bite of her macaroon.

"Well, that sounds nice. You said Jill has two bridesmaids. Will the other one be at the shower too?"

"Yes. Her name is Kristen, and I don't know if I mentioned this, but Kristen and Jeffrey dated too," Maybel said. "She broke Jeffrey's heart. He really liked her. He liked her a lot more than he liked Leah. He has dated so many gals, I have a hard time keeping them straight. I remember Leah because of that Bible story about Jacob having two wives, and he loved Leah less. I use word association. Same thing with Jeffrey and Leah. He loved Leah less than Kristen," Maybel said.

"You mean he loved Leah less than Jill?"

"I think he loved Kristen the most, and he is settling for Jill because he can't have Kristen. He loved Leah the least of all of them," Maybel explained.

Celeste thought if Jeffrey loved Leah the least, this would explain why she seemed to resent Jill.

Maybel continued, "Leah really had it bad for him too, but once Jeffrey met Jill, he forgot all about Leah. But just between you and me, I think Jeffrey still carries a torch for Kristen. He denies it, but a mother knows these things."

Celeste's eyes widened. What a love triangle, she thought. No, wait, there are four of them, so it's a love square, not a triangle. "Jill's two bridesmaids have both dated Jeff? First Kristen, then Leah?"

"They call that carnal knowledge, dear," Maybel said, taking another bite of her macaroon.

Celeste felt like she needed to fasten her seatbelt because she suspected they were in for a bumpy ride.

Chapter Five

Say Cheese

The magazine photoshoot

Jill Jenson was nothing if not beautiful. She possessed her mother's exquisite bone structure and her father's warm chocolate brown eyes. She kept herself in shape by skipping breakfast and performing yoga. When Jill's mother Diane, a former model, found out Jill got engaged, she called in a favor from one of her photographer friends who worked at Bridal Wave magazine. When Diane asked Jacob, the experienced photographer, for the favor, he said, "Oh yes! I've seen pictures of your daughter Jill on social media! She is divine. I'd be happy to talk to the editor at BW and see if we can do a feature on Jill."

Candace Cunningham, the editor of Bridal Wave magazine, knew who Diane Deermark-Jenson was. Candace disliked Diane because years earlier in their careers when Candance was a project manager on a photoshoot for Diane, she found Diane to be stuck up, unrealistic and overly demanding. Despite this, Candace thought it would be interesting to see how a photoshoot with Diane's daughter would turn out. The name alone would draw attention to the magazine. "OK," Candace said to Jacob when he asked, "I'll make sure we have a strong project manager for the shoot. If she's anything like her mother, Jill won't be easy to work with."

Jerri-Anne received Jill's photoshoot assignment. Jerri wasn't from California, and since she moved out to California from Kansas, she'd been obsessed with the beach. When she viewed pictures of Jill, she knew a shoot on the beach would be perfect for her. They would not photograph her in a wedding dress. That had been done to death. Since the photoshoot would be beach themed, Jerri picked out the perfect white sequined bikini from a new designer to make Jill look stunning. Jerri also saw photos of her fiancé Jeffrey and her bridesmaids Kristen and Leah on Jill's social media. Jerri thought it would be fun to include them all.

She did a bit of finagling to talk Jill into it. The brides always want to be photographed by themselves, Jerri thought, but she knew exactly how to persuade Jill into sharing the spotlight. "You're the star of the shoot, and your fiancé and bridesmaids are just the supporting cast," Jerri explained. Jill agreed because she loved the idea of being a star with a supporting cast. Jerri set a date and time for the shoot and continued to arrange everything for it. She lined up Jacob for the photography, and she lined up the hair and make-up artists. She purchased the props for the shoot. When she spoke to Candance about which writer they should use to do Jill's interview, Candace replied, "I'll do it myself."

"Candy, you never write pieces anymore," Jerri said.

"Diane Deermark was such a big name back in the day, I'd love to do this one myself. I want to make sure it's handled properly," Candace explained. She didn't need Jill throwing a fit like her mother used to or giving her magazine a bad name.

"As you wish," Jerri replied, knowing not to cross her boss. She let Candance know the date, time, and location of the shoot.

"Only Jill should wear a bikini, so make sure you pick out one-piece bathing suits for her bridesmaids, and I know the bikini you're using for Jill. It has a sixties spy girl movie feel to it, so make sure the one-piece bathing suits for the bridesmaids have a retro look to them as well. Also, Jacob mentioned Jill has some sort of absurd peacock theme for her wedding, and because of that, the bridesmaids' suits should be purple and aqua blue. We'll mention her wedding theme in the interview. And get some green Hawaiian print swim trunks for her fiancé," Candace instructed Jerri.

"OK, understood. See you at the shoot." Jerri hung up and shopped for the other bathing suits. She quite liked Candance's ideas. That's why she's the editor, Jerri thought as she purchased some retro looking beach chairs, a beach ball and a big umbrella with a peacock on it. She thought these items would give the shoot a fun beach blanket bingo vibe.

In the days prior to the shoot, plans were finalized, and agreements were signed. At the advice of her mother, Jill fasted for the two days prior to the shoot. "You'll be wearing a bikini, and you want your stomach to look as flat as possible," Diane said to her daughter. "It's what I always used to do before any shoot where I was to be photographed in a bathing suit."

The morning of the shoot, a secluded spot on the beach was secured early, and the hair and make-up stations were set up. Jerri managed many shoots in the past and was a pro. Jeffrey showed up first. He breathed in the salt air and hoped this shoot would make Jill happy. He slipped off his flip-flops and walked across the sand, his muscular calves supporting his fast stride. Jerri noticed his broad shoulders and thought he seemed like a nice young man. His hair and make-up only took a few minutes, and she gave him his swim trunks and told him he could change behind the curtain they'd set up. When he came out, Jerri smiled at the sight of his chest. This will be great for the photos, she thought.

Candace showed up next and introduced herself to Jeffrey. She sat down in a director's chair and turned on her iPad. A breeze rustled her hair while she sipped her gourmet coffee from a designer travel mug. Squawking seagulls flew around in the salty air. The breeze chilled her a bit, and she wrapped her plaid pashmina tightly around herself.

Jill arrived after Candance with her mother Diane and her photographer friend Jacob. Jacob quickly scanned the area and decided what angles he'd shoot from first. Diane strode past Candace, not remembering who she was. Candace smiled politely, making note of what Diane looked like now.

Jerri helped Jill get situated with hair and make-up. While Jill fasted in the days prior to the shoot, she also spent some time in the tanning booth. Her skin was bronzed to perfection. She'd made a trip to the beauty salon to get waxed and have more highlights added to her caramel-colored hair.

"If there is another blond in the shoot with you, you want to make sure you are the blondest," Diane instructed, referring to Jill's friend Kristen who also had blond hair. Diane's motherly advice always encouraged narcissism.

The hairdresser combed Jill's hair into an up-do of a tight French twist. "You look like old school Hollywood glamor," she complimented Jill.

The make-up artist brushed some glittery silver eyeshadow onto Jill's lids and glossed her perfect bow shaped mouth with a plum-colored lipstick. Jill frowned when she looked in the mirror. She thought the hairstyle made her look frigid and uptight, and the eye shadow looked garish on her skin tone. Gold would have been better, she thought. The purple tinted lipstick looked deathly on her. Jill expressed her concerns to Jerri, and Jerri replied, "Don't worry about it at all. It's going to photograph so beautifully in the sun! It's very avant-garde!" Jill accepted this answer and sat with Jeffrey. She felt annoyed that

Kristen and Leah were late. Her flat, hungry stomach growled at her and kept her bad mood raging.

Jeffrey sat down next to her on a towel on the sand, remembering the night before. Jill insisted he use one of her expensive hair conditioners so his hair would look good. He happily agreed to do this for her, but when he asked her if he should also use some of her cold cream on his face so his skin would look good, she shouted, "Your *mother* uses cold cream! I use the highest quality *moisturizer* for my skin!"

"I'm sure this photoshoot is going to be amazing!" Jill said to Jeffrey while they waited. "I mean, I can't even take a terrible picture. You've seen my selfies. I don't have a bad side."

Jeffrey nodded.

Jill went on, "I know Leah isn't that photogenic, but at least she is tall and thin. Kristen should look good in the photos, though. She has a great smile almost as great as mine."

Jeffrey wondered what he'd gotten himself into, and it wasn't only the photoshoot. Jill seemed so stuck up now, just like her mother. He wondered why he hadn't seen this before. Deep in thought, a high-pitched scream from Jill jolted him. She spotted a little crab crawling towards them. She jumped back, and Jeffrey carefully grabbed the crab, making sure he didn't get pinched. He took it further away from them, letting it loose and wishing he could crawl away from the photoshoot as well.

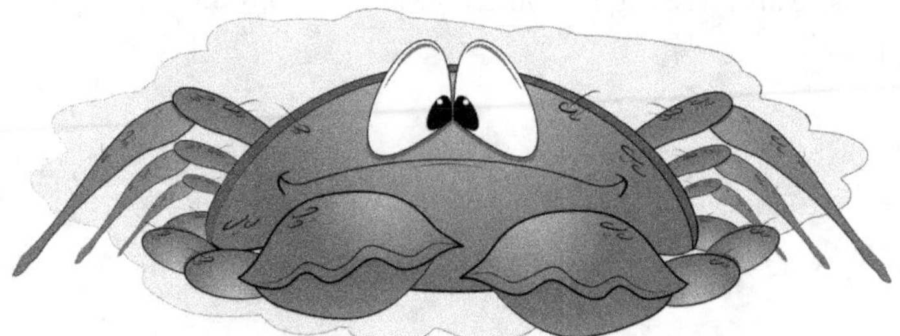

Jeffrey took the crab further away from them, letting it loose and wishing he could crawl away from the photoshoot as well.

Meanwhile, Leah picked Kristen up in her new leased convertible she hoped would impress Kristen. All Kirsten said when she got in was, "I think we're late."

Leah ignored the comment and chatted about all the wonderful features her new car had while she drove along the coast. "I can plug the location into my GPS, and it will guide me there," Leah said.

"You should see my dad's McLaren! Now that's an impressive car! It's the most exhilarating driving experience you can have," Kristen replied, checking her hair in her mirror. "He wanted to get me an orange one, and I said, 'no that's tacky'. So, he's gonna buy me one in blue."

Leah let out a deep breath and slowed down. She was in no hurry to get to the shoot.

Jill got more uptight as each minute passed. When Leah and Kristen finally arrived, Jill shouted at Leah, "What took you so long?!"

Leah flipped her long dark hair back and said, "Don't have a cow, Jill. You said to get here at seven and it's seven now."

"No! I told you that Jacob said to get here at six so we could get ready for the shoot to start at seven and capture the golden hour of morning light! You needed to be here an hour ago!" Rage pumped through Jill's starving body. Of course, Leah would screw up my shoot since she is so jealous of me, Jill thought.

"Oops, I must have misunderstood," Leah said and smiled, "we're here now, and that's all that matters. We're ready for hair and make-up, and speaking of make-up, didn't you tell the make-up artist that purple is not your color? Your lips look bruised."

Jill frowned.

"Oh, and those frown lines," Leah said, shaking her head.

Kristen attempted to keep the mood light and spoke up, "Jill, you look lovely, and that bikini is so couture!"

The make-up artist approached them and called Leah and Kirsten to make-up, saying they'd need to hurry before they lost the morning sunlight. When they emerged, they both looked wonderful. Their eyeliner was winged, their lips were bright red, and their hairstyles were bouffant. They were both given horn-rimmed 1950s style cat-eye shaped sunglasses to wear. The brightly colored retro bathing suits were adorable on them. When Jill saw them, she worried they looked better than her. At least I'm the only one in a bikini, Jill thought, feeling her stomach growl like an angry lion.

Jill's mother Diane had been a pro. No matter how hungry she was during a shoot, it never showed on her face. Jill, on the other hand, was not as experienced. She was never hungry when she took a selfie. Jerri instructed Jill to sit on one of the beach chairs, while Jeffrey stood behind her and was told to nibble on her neck. Leah and Kristen followed instructions to bounce the brightly colored beach ball back and forth between them while they stood in the background behind Jill and Jeffrey. "Oh, fun!" Kristen said, smiling from ear to ear. She obediently tossed the ball to Leah.

Jerri imagined that Jill would giggle when Jeffrey nibbled on her neck. It would make the perfect picture. But Jill did not giggle. She shouted at Jeffrey, "Did you eat onions this morning?! I specifically asked you not to!" Jacob snapped some photos while this argument took place.

"I… I forgot," Jeffrey mumbled and apologized that his breakfast burrito did, in fact, include onions.

Jill let out a disgusted sigh and crossed her arms over her chest, deepening her frown lines.

"Jill, you need to uncross your arms. That won't make for a good photo," Diane coached, "and you need to smile. You're frowning and your frown lines are showing. Try to relax your face and have fun, like Kristen and Leah."

Jacob smiled at Diane, appreciating the help. Diane whispered to Jacob, "Jill doesn't think she has a bad side, but she does. Try to photograph her from the left." Jacob did as he was instructed, and Candace made note of everything she observed.

Jerri gave some instructions and said, "Leah, try to actually catch the beach ball. You keep dropping it and bending over. We only have photos of your rear end. Jeff, why don't you sit next to Jill?"

When Jeffrey tried to get on the beach chair with her, Jill shouted, "She means the beach chair next to me! Not mine!"

A redness crept over Jeffrey's face. Jacob snapped more photos.

Kristen and Leah frolicked in the background, looking wonderful. However, Leah's strapless one-piece bathing suit fit her slim body just a little too loose. It slid down a tad, and she tugged it back into place. Kristen tossed the ball towards Leah, and when Leah's willowy arms shot up in the air while jumping to catch the ball, one of her breasts popped out. "Oops," she said, playfully smiling at Jeffrey and slowly pushing her boob back into the bathing suit.

During the nip slip that ensued, Jeffrey noticed Leah's tan lines. While Jeffrey enjoyed this quick hello from Leah's mammary, Jill screamed at her fiancé, "Stop looking at her!"

Jeffrey tried to protest, but it was no use.

Jill screeched, "It's bad enough my father is always ogling her, but now you too!" Jill's face turned bright red with anger.

Jacob kept snapping pictures through all of this.

Jill's mother Diane sat stiffer than a surfboard. She loved her daughter, but sometimes she was an embarrassment to her, just like her father.

Candace smiled. Jill was just as difficult as her mother. Candance typed away, making more notes.

"OK, let's get a few more shots in while we still have this sweet morning light. All these golden rays of sunshine are hitting everything just right," Jacob said, trying to be positive. "Jeff, why don't you grab Jill's hand and hold it?"

Jeffrey did as he was instructed, but Jill's hand felt cold and was as rigid as her hairstyle. The couple sat in the striped beach chairs holding hands and trying to smile. More shots were snapped, and the smiles looked forced and awkward, despite coaching from Jacob, Jerri, and Diane.

Jacob finally said, "Alright, I think we've got some good shots. Let's call it a day. Thank you, everyone."

Diane knew they didn't have very many good shots, but there was nothing else she could do. Despite Diane's coaching, the photoshoot turned out to be a disaster. She worried it would reflect badly on her name. At least I'm not in any of these bad shots, she thought while gathering up her stuff. She left without saying goodbye to anyone. Jill would need to stay longer to be interviewed by Candace for the magazine article and would get a ride home with Jeffrey.

Driving home, Diane Deermark-Jenson thought more about the day. Her daughter Jill got her good looks, but she'd gotten her father's brains and temperament. This was not a good thing, in Diane's opinion. Diane gave up so much for her husband and daughter. She'd given up her modeling career to be a wife and a mother, and all the money she'd earned as a model went into the family business. Now, her husband put her on a tight budget. This made her burn inside every time she thought about it.

Her daughter had an unrealistic dream about being an actress, but for the time being, she was selling tacky jewelry for the family business. While Diane knew Jill tried her best to design jewelry, she also knew Jill's designs stunk. They were gaudy at best. Despite her frustrations, Diane loved her family and would do anything she could to help them.

Pulling into the driveway of their million-dollar home mortgaged to the hilt, she hoped her friend Jacob would be able to edit the photos to make at least one of them work. She also hoped Jill wouldn't put her foot in her mouth for the magazine interview. This hope was futile.

When Candace asked Jill what she was looking forward to most about married life, Jill replied, "His complete and total unconditional love for me! I'm trying to become an actress in Hollywood and I need his full support."

Candace titled her head to the side and asked, "What about your unconditional love for him? Have you thought about what that will take?"

Jill frowned and heard the waves crashing hard on the shore behind her. After a long pause, she lied and said, "Of course."

Candace smiled and asked, "And what do you think it will take?"

"Cooperation," Jill replied, feeling proud of how smart her answer was.

"Will you elaborate on that?" Candace prodded.

"As long as he does what I want and cooperates, we won't have any problems. Jeff usually does what I say, but sometimes he doesn't and I have to get real strict with him," Jill answered.

Candace smiled, making more notes.

Chapter Six

A Cog in the Machine

"What do you mean, it's broken?" Jack Jenson asked, frown lines displaying his disapproval to his subordinate.

"The hollow pipe making machine keeps jamming every time we try to make this new design of Jill's. I think it broke our machine. We're going to need a new one," John Swormy, Jack's lead technician, answered nervously. "Jill's designs aren't practical like Leah's. Jill puts holes in the wrong spots, and these stones she gave us to inset into her design keep cracking, and the hollow pipe making machine is for…well, pipe. It won't work on these silver studs she asked us to make."

Jack shook his proud head and said, "No. There is no money in the budget for a new machine. It's your job to run the line, so figure it out and fix it!" He waved his hand back and forth like a flapping, windblown sail on a boat, motioning for John to leave his office.

"Yes, sir. Whatever you say." Walking out, John Swormy wondered what he was going to do. He went back to the machine to take another look at it. After tinkering with it for a few minutes, he got it working again, but he decided to hand-make Jill's jewelry so as not to break the machine again. No one is going to buy this crap anyway, he thought. He wound metal pieces around with his plyers and glued stones into place.

The smell of salt air wafted into Jack's office from the open window behind his enormous oak desk. Seagulls squawked, flying around the harbor, picking up scraps of beach goers' lunches. He buzzed Leah and asked her to come to his office.

One extra button on her silk blouse was unbuttoned first. Leah got up from her desk, hurrying to Jack's office. "You rang?" She smiled.

"Please, have a seat," Jack ordered, pointing to the chair on the other side of his desk. "John said they're having trouble with the hollow pipe making machine. He said Jill's designs are causing it to jam or something. Can you take a look at them?" He pushed Jill's designs that had been amateurishly sketched out on graph paper towards Leah.

Leah studied them closely and suppressed a giggle. Garbage, she thought. She craned her long skinny neck to the side, and her scapulas arched back like wings. "I'm not really sure what I can do about these… and is this a chicken?"

"No, it's a peacock, I think," Jack answered.

Leah leaned in towards Jack. "You know, I went to design school for years to learn how to do what I do. I'm not sure why Jill thinks she can suddenly design jewelry. She should stick to sales."

Jack let out a heavy steamboat of a sigh. "I know."

"I mean, it's not as simple as just drawing an idea on paper. You must truly think about the practicality of the design, while still making it creative and delicate. Then, you must think about the materials you are going to use, price them out, and lastly, you need to make sure they can be created on the machinery. It's a very involved process. These earrings aren't too bad, but I saw the stones she gave to John to make them out of. They aren't the right type of material for this design. John's machinery will crack those stones in a second." Leah flipped her long hair back and smiled at Jack.

"We cut jade all the time. Maybe this is just bad luck," Jack said.

"John does that manually using diamond wire handsaw blades," Leah explained, "and it's very time consuming, making it an expensive product. I don't think Jill's design would warrant a high-end price."

"I'm going to need for you to coach Jill on her designs," Jack said, sailing a hand through his thinning hair.

"Coach her? You mean like teach her how to do what I do?" Leah frowned. "Jack, like I said, it took me years to learn how to do what I do. I can't just teach it to her. Besides, I'm not sure she really has the knack for it. I know Jill is used to always getting what she wants, but this may be the one thing she needs to let go."

"Then I'll need for you to tell her to stick to sales," Jack said. "We need more sales, anyway. Just let her know I'll have John hand-make a few demos of what she designed, but we can't mass produce all of them right now. We just don't have the resources. Maybe we can manufacture the turquoise jewelry if you'll work with John. Maybe you can adjust the design so he can manufacture it. Will you at least meet with him and see what you guys can come up with?"

She gave her agreement and bobbed her head like a buoy in the ocean. When she returned to her shared office with Jill and sat down at her desk, Jill inquired, "What was that about? What did my dad want?"

Knowing Jill would loath the answer, Leah smirked and informed Jill, "Jack said to tell you to stick to sales. Your designs aren't practical, and he can't mass produce them. He asked *me* to fix them."

Tears lined the bottom of Jill's long-lashed eyes. She'd worked for hours on those designs and thought they were quite good. She protested, "I'd rather not have my designs produced at all than let you touch them!"

"I saw the receipts, Jill." Leah stared at her business partner.

"So?" Jill flipped her long blond hair back.

"Remember our little agreement about what you're doing," Leah said, logging off her computer. She clutched her designer bag and breezed out.

Jill sat at her desk with rage blasting out of her like a foghorn. Who did Leah think she was? She wouldn't even have this job if it weren't for her and her family. Jill didn't know what to do, so she did what she always did when she didn't know what to do. She went straight to daddy.

Jack logged off his computer and said, "Sweetie, I don't have time to talk right now. I've got a lunch appointment to get to."

"But Daddy," Jill begged, "I really need to speak to you about a serious problem."

Jack closed his window, cutting off the breeze. "OK pumpkin, tonight we'll chat, and I'll figure it all out for you."

Chapter Seven

Showering the Bride

Saturday March 17, 2018
(Jill's wedding shower and St. Patrick's Day)

Maybel lovingly decorated the old Rec room by carefully covering the tables with peacock-colored tablecloths. She assembled and set out paper foldouts of peacocks on each table. Next, she placed purple petunia plants festively in the center of each table. She sprinkled bright green confetti around it all. She tied helium-filled balloons in various places in the Rec room and hung streamers from the ceiling beams with care.

After the food table was ready to go, Maybel tasked Celeste with putting out the candy dishes of mints and Jordan almonds at each table. In Maybel's opinion, they were a must have at any wedding or baby shower.

Jill screeched at her mom standing in the corner of the Regal Palms Rec room. "She's wearing white, mother!"

While Celeste arranged the nuts and mints, she heard Jill's mom Diane say to her, "At least this isn't your wedding. It's only your shower." Celeste knew they were talking about Leah, her maid of honor, chief bridesmaid, and business partner. She showed up wearing an extremely short, white, strapless dress. She brought the fixings for Sangria. Leah set out five bottles of wine, a Tupperware container of cut up fruit and two pitchers on the food table. Maybel rushed over to help Leah put the Sangria together. Once the chopped fruit was drenched in cheap wine, Leah poured herself a big glass and sat down at one of the tables.

Celeste greeted her and let her know her realtor was having an open house at her condo the next day.

Leah's long pointy black fingernails typed away, and then she looked up and Celeste and asked, "What?"

Celeste explained, "At Jill's engagement dinner, you mentioned you wanted to check out my place since I'm selling it."

"You're the one that sat next to that hot guy at Jeff and Jill's engagement dinner," Leah said. "I'll try to swing by tomorrow." Leah went back to her phone and drank more wine.

Guests filtered into the Rec room, and Celeste stepped away from Leah quickly. The room filled with young women bearing gifts wrapped in beautiful paper and tied with fluffy bows. Maybel and Celeste directed the ladies to put them down on a gift table set up in the corner. The room got loud with chatter, and Jill, also in a slinky white dress, made her way around the room, greeting everyone.

Maybel explained the rules for the games, and Celeste passed out the plastic rings and rolls of toilet paper. As she did, Kristen introduced herself to Celeste.

When the wholesome, sunny looking girl greeted Celeste, it became obvious to her that Kristen's mother taught her manners. She wore a flowy peach floral sundress, and it made her skin look like the color of rosé wine. "Do you need help with anything? I feel bad I couldn't help out ahead of time for the shower, but I had to work. That's also why I couldn't make the engagement dinner."

On first impression, Celeste liked Kristen a lot more than Leah or Jill, for that matter. "I think it's almost game time," Celeste said, motioning to Maybel. "Thank you for offering, though. Maybe you can help with cleanup."

Kristen's bright face beamed with a smile. "Sounds great!"

"Alright ladies! Keep your ears open for the keywords 'wedding' or 'bride', and if you hear someone say it, you can take away their ring. But in the meantime, we are going to play another game. We will need for you to break up into teams of two. Each team will get a few rolls of toilet paper. You'll need someone in your group to volunteer to be the bride—"

"I get your ring!" Leah shouted.

"Here," Maybel said, quickly handing it to Leah, hoping that would shut her up. "Each team will need to cover the bride in a toilet paper wedding dress. Jill will pick her favorite as the winner. Now go!"

Everyone scurried around, forming teams to get started. High-pitched giggles filled the room while shower attendees were covered in strips of toilet paper from head to toe. Their partners frantically covered them up the best they could. One team made little roses out of the toilet paper and attached them to their dress, while another team made a veil out of toilet paper. One young lady with toilet paper fastened to her head asked her partner to tie toilet paper bows to her shoes.

Leah put her third glass of sangria down long enough to get creative with her dress. Diligently, she worked the toilet paper around Kristen's body, covering it with a crisscross pattern. She twisted pieces of toilet paper, expertly making a necklace and bracelet for her partner Kristen.

When the time was up, Jill went around checking each one. The teams laughed at each other while Jill picked the dress Leah's team designed as the winner. Maybel handed Leah a bottle of sparkling Italian wine as her prize.

"Are we supposed to share it?" Leah asked Maybel loudly.

"It's OK, Leah. You take it," Kristen said, smiling with toilet paper clinging to her body. She looked down at herself. "This dress is almost as short as the one Jill is wearing!"

After the game, food was served. Guests made their way through the food line, dishing up slices of vegan pizza and cold chickpea salad with diced cucumber, mint, and cilantro. Maybel brewed a carafe of coffee to accompany the gluten-free strawberry tarts. She walked around with a tray of the glazed tarts, offering them to the ladies. Everyone took one except Kristen, who said she was allergic to strawberries. She munched on the Jordan almonds instead.

Celeste noticed Leah opened the gift bottle of wine and began swigging from it. She thought about warning Leah that she could ruin a friendship if she drank too much, but instead she took Maybel aside and said, "I think we should have Jill open gifts soon, because Leah is getting trashed."

Maybel agreed and asked Jill to move over to the gift table. The first gift she opened was a white lace nightie. "That's from me!" Kristen said. Jill went on to open more gifts of various types of lingerie. Celeste noticed Maybel seemed a little uncomfortable. Then, Jill opened Maybel's gift - a crock pot.

At this point during the shower, Leah had consumed enough alcohol to loosen her mouth liberally. She shouted, "Now you can slow cook Jeff some carrots! Just what every man wants!"

The guests giggled, and Maybel pursed her lips. "Well, Jill, in my day, when we had a wedding shower, we gave gifts for your pantry, not panties," Maybel said, defending her gift. She straightened out her blouse as if they were feathers that got ruffled.

"Here, open mine," Celeste said, handing her gift to Jill. Not able to bring herself to get Jill lingerie, Celeste picked out a vegan soy scented candle set for her instead. A variety of fruity scented wax was nestled in beveled glass votive candle holders.

When Jill held up Celeste's gift, Leah blurted out, "Mood lighting for when Jeff does his signature move!" Leah threw her head back, laughing.

Celeste looked over at Jill's mother Diane, and Diane's perfectly high cheek bones turned a deep shade of red from her disapproval. Kristen tried to quiet Leah down, but that seemed to only annoy Leah and make her worse. Jill continued to open gifts, saying thank you as she went. If Leah's behavior bothered Jill, Jill did not show it.

Celeste took Maybel aside and asked, "How are we going to get Leah home? She's too drunk to drive."

"I can ask Vick to drive her home," Maybel suggested, taking out her phone to text him.

Jill continued to open presents. She was gifted bras, panties, garters, nighties, thongs, and a book from Leah on the Kama Sutra. When Jill opened it, Leah said loudly, "That's my gift. Now Jeff can learn a new signature move!" Leah laughed so hard she almost fell out of her chair.

Jill burned inside, hotter than the soy candle set would have. She faked a laugh and opened another gift. Leah's intoxication kept her from realizing the damage she did.

Vick entered the Rec room, his prematurely balding head almost touching the door frame. Vick pictured himself on the right side of political justice, but really, he was just an asshole. He played the political game better than Maybel, and for that, Maybel could barely stand him. "Hello ladies! I'm Vick, President of the Regal Palms HOA," he said, waving and nodding to the room. Instantly, he spotted empty wine bottles on the food table, turned to Maybel and told her, "Maybel, you know you're not supposed to serve alcohol in the Rec room. It's against the HOA rules."

"I didn't serve it. Leah brought it. I didn't know she was going to bring alcohol," Maybel replied. She cleared her throat and went on, "I'm glad to see you're able to walk normally now after that freak accident you had in the summer."

"It wasn't an accident. I was attacked by a maniac, and you know it. A lesser man would not have survived what I survived. You would have died *immediately*. The fact that I survived proves I'm unbeatable," Vick retorted and continued, "and don't change the subject. You know you are not supposed to serve alcohol in the Rec room. You're in big trouble!"

"I know the rules, Vick. I helped write the bylaws for Regal Palms while you were still soiling every one of your diapers, and your mommy was still wiping snot from your nose! As I said, I didn't bring the alcohol. Leah did," Maybel said.

Vick asked which one Leah was, and Maybel motioned to Leah, who had moved over to the gift table. She wiggled around, holding up one of the bras to her own chest. Vick's eyebrows raised as he fixed his gaze on her. "Well, hello momma," he murmured under his breath.

"She's going to need a ride home," Maybel said.

Vick uttered, "I'll caravan that all day long." With his engine revved, Vick quickly motored towards Leah, a trail of lusty exhaust emanating from his libido as he traveled over to the long, lanky female.

Maybel turned to Celeste and asked, "Dear, was that book Leah gave Jill an instruction book on the sex?"

Jill approached Maybel and Celeste, making Celeste feel relieved she didn't have to answer Maybel's question. "Maybel, I just wanted to thank you again for the shower. It was so nice of you to host it in this old… charming Rec room." Jill forced a polite smile.

Maybel warmly smiled back and said, "Oh, no trouble at all, Jill. You're almost family now."

Jill held up a big pink bag and said, "I have some gifts for you, Kristen, Leah and Celeste." She called Kristen and Leah over.

Leah swayed and stumbled towards them. Vick caught her arm and then anchored her hips, fondling her bosom while he tried to help her stay upright. Leah giggled at Vick. Closing her eyes, her head flopped back like a newborn baby. She slurred, "You're so tall!"

Vick wondered if he might get lucky when her rear end bumped into his crotch.

Maybel snapped, "Vick! Bring Leah over here!"

Once everyone gathered, Jill began, "As you know, Leah and I have a jewelry business called Jaded Edge. Normally, Leah does all the jewelry designs, and I handle the sales. But recently, I've started designing my own jewelry, too. As a thank you to all of you for being so kind to me and helping with all the wedding stuff, I've designed some special jewelry for each of you. I was hoping you could all wear these pieces to my wedding! They've all been handmade, especially for each of you."

"Oh, how lovely," Maybel said.

Jill pulled out four boxes from her pink bag and began handing them out. Kristen opened hers first. A pair of purple rose pedal earrings and matching hair clip were in her box. Jill explained to Kristen, "I know purple roses are your favorite. Jeff mentioned that one time."

"Yeah, he used to give me…," Kristen stopped herself from going on. The group knew Kristen was going to say Jeff used to give her purple roses. Even Leah, who was plastered knew this. Celeste saw Leah snarl at the remark and then hiccup, or maybe the hiccup forced the snarl. Celeste wasn't sure. "Jill, I love them. Thank you." Kristen smiled sweetly. Jill frowned at the realization as to why Jeff knew purple roses were her favorite. She felt foolish for not connecting the dots sooner.

Leah opened her box next. A shiny silver lip ring and matching tongue ring sat in her box. Each of them had a decorative round ball stud attached to it. "The design is so simple. These round ball studs attached to the rings look like those starter earrings you get at the mall for little girls." Leah laughed. "I can't wait to wear them. They're so edgy," Leah sputtered, and Celeste suspected she was being sarcastic.

"Edgy like you, my friend," Jill said, forcing another smile and went on, "We both know you give the edge to Jaded Edge. Maybel, open yours!" Jill handed over another box.

Maybel's box, bigger than the others, revealed a hideous, giant metal peacock necklace with big green, blue, and purple stones along where the feathers would be. It hung from a thick chain and included a hair clip with real peacock feathers on it. "Oh, my… how interesting," Maybel said, holding up the necklace. Celeste knew this was Maybel's polite tone. Everyone stared at the necklace like a train wreck, unable to look away from the tacky, jeweled peacock.

"Ugh, gawd! I like my toilet paper jewelry better than that thing!" Leah blurted out, laughing.

Jill ignored Leah and said, "Maybel, the green, purple, and blue stones on your peacock necklace are real jade from Canada. I picked those beads out special for you."

Thinking she was going to look like an idiot, Maybel continued to use her polite tone and said, "Thank you, dear. This was so thoughtful of you. I can't wait to wear it."

Jill turned to Celeste and smiled. "Celeste, please open yours."

Celeste nervously opened her box. With relief, she took her items out of the box, a black choker and a turquoise beaded hair comb. The black choker had a white cameo on the front and a little delicate thin chain at the fastener designed to hang down the back of your neck. She could handle this, she thought and said, "These are so nice. Thank you!" Celeste hugged Jill.

"Those are real turquoise beads from Mexico on your hair comb. I tried to make jewelry for everyone that really represented them. I picked this cameo for you because of your porcelain skin," Jill said to Celeste.

Maybel wondered how the heck a peacock represented her.

"What jewelry are you going to wear?" Celeste asked Jill.

"Oh, I had a copper necklace made for me. It has two handwritten J's on it joined together with a diamond, you know, for Jeff and Jill," Jill explained.

Leah spouted out, "Or for Jill Jenson."

Jill looked a little embarrassed and said, "Well, Leah is right. I had it made before I met Jeff, but it's still perfect for us! Nothing wrong with repurposing it."

Shortly after the presentation of the jewelry, guests trickled out of the Rec room. Vick placed his hand on Leah's long, skinny arm and steered her out towards her car, which was parked across the street in the covered parking lot. She wobbled along, hanging onto his hairy forearm. He asked where she parked, and she raised her hand and pointed towards the north end of the lot. When they got to her car, Vick propped Leah up against the car while he unlocked the door and opened it. Right before she slid down the side of her car, he caught her and guided her into the passenger seat. "Do you have a signature move?" she asked Vick, giggling. He clipped the seatbelt into place and got in on the driver's side.

Vick was eager to drive Leah to her over-priced apartment, but being much taller than Leah, he could barely fit behind the driver's seat, so he had to shove the seat back. Once on the road, he fumbled around, trying to put the top down. Leah hardly knew where she was. She popped one eye open to see him driving down the highway that ran along the ocean. Her new leased convertible was stick shift, and Vick hadn't driven stick since he was in high school. The herky-jerky ride coupled with Leah's intoxication made her head fling around like a pinball when he shifted from gear to gear.

"Ooooh… I think I'm going to be sick," she moaned.

"Can you hold out a little longer? We're almost to your place," Vick said, racing along the street. He saw a spot by her building and down shifted roughly to parallel park into it. When he did this, Leah hurled her vegan bridal shower lunch all over the car.

Vick turned the car off and ran around to her side and helped her get out. They ambled up the stairs to her second-floor apartment, and he unlocked her door. Leah was still groaning from intoxication overload. Vick led her to her couch, and she collapsed on it. He grabbed a blue blanket that was hanging on the back of the couch and wiped her vomit off his forearm with it. He pulled her shoes off and covered her with the blanket. He used the app on his phone to request an Uber ride back to Regal Palms, later billing Maybel for the ride.

Meanwhile, Kristen had stuck around to help Maybel and Celeste clean up, while Diane helped Jill load all the gifts into her car. When they were cleaning up, Kristen struck up a conversation with Celeste. "It was so nice of Maybel to do this for Jill. I thought Leah, as the maid of honor, should have done it."

Celeste threw some paper cups away and said, "I think Leah doesn't have the budget for it."

"Maybe, but there are other things Leah should be doing that she's not, like the toast at the wedding. She should be doing it, but she asked me to do it. I think it's because Leah is still hung up on Jeff and can't stomach it. Clearly, I'm over him, so I agreed to do it," Kristen went on with a giggle. "Jill and Leah always salivate over my leftovers."

"That's sweet of you to do the toast. Not everyone likes public speaking," Celeste pointed out.

"Yeah, everyone says I'm the sweet one in the group, and they're right," Kristen continued, "I may not be the sweetest person around, but I'm definitely not as sour as Leah." Kristen put some more paper plates in the trashcan and turned back to Celeste saying, "Well, I've got to get going. I have a hot date tonight. It was so nice to meet you, and I'll see you at the wedding." Kristen waved and walked out of the Regal Palms Rec room.

Glad the shower was over, Celeste wondered how it ended up feeling even more awkward than the engagement dinner. The wedding was next, but it couldn't possibly be as bad as the shower, she thought.

Chapter Eight

The Luck of the Irish

The day after Jill's wedding shower, Celeste's realtor, Traci, set up an open house at her condo. That meant Celeste could not be home. She nervously took a big step and texted Brian to see how he was doing, and he asked her if she wanted to meet for lunch that day. After doing some shopping, she met him at an Irish pub by Regal Palms. Because it was St. Patrick's Day weekend, they offered a special on corned beef & cabbage and shepherd's pie. This food paired well with the dark beer they ordered. They sat in a secluded corner booth decorated in dark wood and lucky horseshoes. A small vase of green carnations bloomed at the edge of the table, next to the salt and pepper shakers.

"I don't understand how you make a dress out of toilet paper," Brian said, with a mouth full of potatoes. "Wouldn't it rip?"

"They weren't actual dresses," Celeste explained. "Leah won the contest, but she got super drunk. Maybel had to ask Vick to drive her home."

Brian buttered a piece of rye bread. "Vick texted me and told me he took some hottie home, but I didn't know who he was talking about. He said she was really drunk and threw up chunks of mango and garbanzo beans. He said it shot out all over the dashboard, and he wasn't sure if he was smelling stomach acid or feta cheese, but he didn't care because it wasn't his car."

Celeste asked, "You and Vick text?"

"Yeah, we're buddies. We even went to a *Lakers* game… and speaking of *Lakers*, I can't believe you're wearing that shirt," Brian said, taking a swig of his ale.

That day, Celeste wore an old, faded *Boston Celtics* t-shirt she bought in Boston while attending an insurance conference there years earlier. "What? It's in honor of St. Patrick's day. It has a little leprechaun on it."

Brian shook his head. "Normally, I'd be secretly checking out your chest, but I can't even look at you in that shirt," he said.

Celeste laughed. "OK, duly noted."

"You said Jill gave you all jewelry? That was nice." Brian held up his empty beer mug to the server, indicating he wanted another one. "You want another one?"

"No, one is my limit. And yes, Jill gave us all jewelry. It was nice of her, but Maybel's necklace is really ugly. I feel bad to say it, but thank God she didn't give me that peacock necklace. She wants us all to wear our jewelry to the wedding, and she made us color coordinate with the peacock colors. Maybel is wearing forest green. Leah is wearing purple. Kristen is wearing teal, and I'm wearing aqua blue," Celeste explained.

"Teal? What is that?" Brian asked.

"It's a color somewhere between blue and green," Celeste explained.

"I'm a bit color blind," Brian admitted.

"Speaking of color," Celeste went on, "apparently Jeff used to give Kristen purple roses when they were dating, which is why they are her favorite. As awkward as the engagement dinner was, I think the shower was worse. Jill designed purple rose earrings for Kristen, but it seemed she didn't realize Jeff used to give purple roses to Kristen when they were dating."

Frowning, Brian asked, "Why purple? Is there some sort of special meaning? It's such a waste to give women flowers."

"Purple roses symbolize love at first sight. Some men give women flowers because they think it will help them get lucky." Celeste pulled the napkin off her lap and set it on the table.

"You can get lucky without giving a woman flowers. Are you going to finish your corned beef?" Brian asked, and Celeste shook her head, pushing her plate towards him. He dug into the morsels left on her plate. "How do you know what purple roses symbolize?"

"I've read things about what different colored roses symbolize. White roses symbolize purity, and red roses are for passion. Orange roses symbolize admiration. They're a way of saying you're proud of someone, and their fiery color is considered to have their own exciting energy. The number of roses you give to someone also has meaning. For example, three roses means I love you, four roses mean nothing will come between us, seven roses mean you are infatuated with someone, eight roses is to show support for a family member going through a difficult time, and thirteen roses mean friends forever. That's why I give Ronnie thirteen roses on her birthday–pink ones because they symbolize sweetness and femininity."

"Is there a quiz on this later? The only thing I remember is the nuns talking about the rose of Sharon, but I barely remember what that meant."

"Rose of Sharon is a hibiscus, not a rose, and it has spiritual meaning, symbolizing the coming of Christ," Celeste explained, squeezing the wedge of lemon into her water.

"I think you paid more attention than I did at school. I thought they were talking about some lady's garden," Brian said.

"I didn't want to get cracked on the knuckles with the ruler," Celeste teased.

"I developed early onset arthritis from all the trouble I got into in school."

"Vick didn't take advantage of Leah, did he?" Celeste asked, circling back to that topic.

"Nah, he said he made sure she got into her apartment, covered her with a blanket, and took an Uber home." Brian started on his second beer.

Celeste changed the subject, fishing around for information. "Speaking of car rides, Maybel seems to think that back in the summer when that maniac who lived at Regal Palms attacked Vick with his own car… that in that attack… Vick's man parts were… crushed."

"I don't know. We don't talk about his fun bits. Vick did say he got an invitation to the wedding, so it sounds like he'll get another shot at Leah," Brian said, flipping the subject back on Celeste.

"Yeah, Maybel said because her and Jeff don't have much family of their own, Diane said she could invite a few friends. She also invited my friend Ronnie who's bringing Tom," Celeste said, referring to Tom Fitzpatrick, another Regal Palms HOA board member who had been dating her best friend Veronica Morgan since they met at last year's Halloween party.

"She was the alligator, right?"

Celeste smiled. "She might have been a crocodile. There is no way to be certain."

After lunch, Brian and Celeste strolled down the road to an Italian Ice stand on the main highway that ran along the beach. Celeste wasn't hungry but couldn't go back to her place yet. Brian, however, ordered a mango tango swirled with peaches and cream. They sat at one of the picnic tables outside the stand that faced the ocean. Chunky clouds spattered across the sky, and a pleasant breeze pushed the clouds around and fluffed Celeste's long hair. She pulled off her 1980s style neon green framed sunglasses that matched her t-shirt and looked out at the ocean, remembering the boat she would have to board for the wedding. She took a deep breath and put her sunglasses back on.

"What's wrong? You look worried," Brian asked, spooning his frozen dessert. The gold rims of his aviator sunglasses sparkled in the California afternoon sunlight.

"Nothing… you'll think I'm crazy if I tell you," Celeste responded.

Brian poked his elbow into Celeste's side and said, "I already think you're crazy, so you might as well tell me."

Celeste chuckled. "I haven't been in or on the ocean since I was a kid. I have a fear of sharks. I saw *Jaws* when I was a kid and never got over it."

"We're gonna need a bigger boat," Brian said.

"What?" Celeste asked.

"Do you think Jeff is making a mistake?" Brian asked.

"Why do you ask that?"

"That's not an answer, Celeste." Brian had a bit of brain freeze from his Italian ice.

"Do *you* think he's making a mistake?" Celeste asked.

"I asked you first," Brian said, smiling.

"I don't know. It's not for me to say. I know Maybel thinks there's something off about Jill, but don't moms always have a hard time with their daughter in laws?"

"I think it's men that have a hard time with their mother in laws." Brian scraped up the last of his fruity iced treat.

"Just in laws in general, huh?" Celeste felt the cold from the ocean breeze, and cars raced by on the coast highway behind them.

"I had great mother in laws. I got along with them better than their daughters," Brian said.

Thinking of Brian's two ex-wives reminded Celeste, and she asked, "Did I mention that both of Jill's bridesmaids dated Jeff?"

Brian laughed. "No. I would have remembered that. Oh man, this wedding is going to be a lot of fun."

Celeste looked at Brian and said, "You know, I hate to be negative, but Jill, Leah, and Kristen, all remind me of paper dolls."

"Paper dolls?"

"Yeah," Celeste said, "when I was a little girl, I played with paper dolls. You could mix and match their clothes and accessories, which was fun, but they were so one dimensional and fragile because they could rip easily. It wasn't like playing with real dolls, but they always looked perfect."

"You lost me, kid," Brian said.

Celeste took a deep breath and looked out at the ocean. The sea foam bubbled and curdled at the shoreline from the rolling waves. "I don't know. There is just something so shallow about them, especially Jill and Leah. How was your Italian ice?"

"Scrumptious! Just like the company," Brian answered, winking.

"That's a good line," Celeste said, rubbing her arms to stay warm.

"It's not a line. You gotta cut me some slack."

"What?" Celeste frowned.

"You're closed off, Celeste," Brian said gently, "you keep me at a distance. You're sitting right here next to me, but I still feel like there is an ocean between us. I think you're afraid I'll hurt you."

Celeste remembered Dr. Fisher's homework assignment. She was to act out of love and not fear. She pushed the assignment out of her head. She always hated doing homework. "Your tongue is bright orange from the ice. It's hard to take you seriously."

"Orange… wasn't that the color for admiration?"

Celeste nodded.

"Well, then, how appropriate. Since I do admire you." Brian leaned over and licked the side of Celeste's face with his ice-cold, orange-stained tongue.

Celeste giggled and knew that wasn't a line. She reached for his hand to get closer.

"Your hand is freezing," he said.

"You know what they say, cold hands, warm heart."

Walking back towards Regal Palms, Brian asked Celeste how the sale of her condo was going. Her phone binged, and she checked it. "This is my realtor. She needs to give me a briefing about how the open house went. Also, she wanted to tell me about a few new places she thinks I'll like."

"Alright, alright. I got the hint," he said, hugging her. "Do you want me to pick you up for the wedding? Or do you have to get to the boat early?"

"I promised Maybel I would help her. Jill asked her to do an appetizer for the wedding. I'll need to help Maybel load everything up in my car and get there ahead of time to set things up," Celeste explained.

"OK, I'll meet you on the boat then. And you know, there's a three-date rule."

"I'm not bound by your rules." She tilted her head and smiled. "Don't be late, or we'll have to leave without you," Celeste warned.

Brian saluted her. "Vick and I will be there on time. Don't you worry your pretty little head about it," Brian said, kissed her cheek, and said goodbye. Celeste smelled the sweet mango on his breath.

Her realtor, Traci, waited for her when she got back. She sat on one of Celeste's purple barstools, looking at her phone. "Good news! There were at least two interested and qualified buyers that showed up today. There were also a few lookie loos, but that's to be expected. I think you'll get an offer soon. Here, sit down so I can show you a few listings I think will be perfect for you," Traci said, pulling out the barstool next to her.

Celeste looked over the print outs Traci handed her. They were much closer to her work and in her price range. "I'll look at these online too, so I can see the pictures better. If I like them, how about we go look at them soon?" Celeste asked. Traci put her phone down and nodded her head. The sun shining through the windows made Traci's long red hair look like flames burning down her back. Celeste admired and respected Traci for being good at her job—another fiercely independent woman, like Celeste.

About a half hour after Traci left, there was a knock at Celeste's door. She assumed it was Maybel, but she was wrong. "Hello, Leah. How are you?" Celeste smiled politely.

"I have a bit of a headache, but other than that, I'm OK. Sorry I'm late. I lost track of time," Leah apologized, walking in. Her tight black leggings paired with a flowy green and white blouse and ankle boots made her look perfectly stylish, no outward sign of a hangover except for slightly bloodshot eyes hidden behind Jackie-O style sunglasses.

Oh, to be in your 30s and be able to bounce back that quick, Celeste thought. Leah's usual thin gold lip ring around her plump bottom lip made Celeste wonder if she'd had her lips injected with collagen. Beautiful diamond leaf earrings dangled from her lobes, and a brilliant green jade bracelet encircled her tiny wrist. Celeste asked if Leah designed those jewelry pieces herself, finding out she had.

"Well, this is my place. Feel free to look around," Celeste invited.

Leah did just that, walking around the entire condo and stopping to look closely at everything. Regal Palms was built in the 1950s, but Celeste's place had been remodeled. "What a magnificent view!" Leah commented on the best part of Celeste's condo, an awesome view of downtown Sunshine Beach. She seemed to like the place. Celeste wondered if she was serious about buying.

"If you're interested, I can give you my realtor's number, and you can contact her," Celeste said. She handed Leah one of Traci's business cards. Leah tossed it in her designer purse. "How fun was that wedding shower yesterday?" Celeste wasn't sure why she asked Leah that. It wasn't fun. It was awkward.

"I always hate things like that," Leah replied.

Celeste wondered if she meant wedding showers or getting drunk and throwing up all over her car. "That was nice of Vick to make sure you got home safely," Celeste prodded.

"To be honest, I don't really remember. I mean, I vaguely recall some really tall dude helping me up the stairs, but after that, it gets fuzzy," Leah said, looking out at Celeste's view again. She turned back around and faced Celeste. "Can I ask you something?"

"Sure."

"Do you really think Jeff loves Jill?" Leah's lazy looking eyes stared at Celeste, waiting for a response.

Celeste blinked a few times. "Uh, I would think so. I don't really know him or Jill that well, though."

"I just can't believe he's really in love with Jill. You know, I dated him before Jill did, and we had a really great thing going. I'm as pretty as Jill. I don't know what Jeff thinks she has that I don't have.

"I even helped Jeff get over Kristen. And don't be fooled by Kristen, she's not as sweet as she pretends to be. Jeff never gave me purple roses, but do you know why he didn't? He told me that Kristen laughed at them when he gave them to her and accused him of being too cheap to buy red ones. She emotionally scarred him. He never wanted to give flowers to a woman again… and even though he never gave me purple roses, I know he cared for me, but then, out of nowhere, he broke up with me. When he was on duty, he happened to go out on a call at her stupid cooking class, and that's how they met. Then, when she found out he'd been dating me, she dangled him in front of me like a prize. And I know this isn't my place to say, but Kristen told me that Jeff told her that Jill is boring in bed, and he doesn't know why he's with her." Leah let out a sigh, flipping her hair back. "Ugh, she's always been so competitive with me."

"Always?" Celeste asked.

"Yeah, we've been friends since college. She always tried to outdo me; always thought she was better than me because she comes from money. Now, she is even trying to design jewelry. That's always been my thing. Her jewelry is horrible, too. I've seen all her designs. They suck. I can't believe Jack signed off on them. He doesn't want her to throw a fit, so he just goes along with it. John, the jewelry maker, even came to me to ask for help with her designs. They're so bad. And can I tell you something else?" Leah asked.

Celeste nodded.

Leah leaned in a little and whispered, "Jill is a psycho."

All this information took Celeste aback, and she wasn't sure what to say. It felt as if the air in the room stunk with all the piles of dirty laundry Leah had just stacked up. After a pause, Celeste spoke carefully, "I know you really liked Jeff, but you're a beautiful girl. You'll meet someone else. I'm sure of it."

"How about that hot guy that was at the engagement dinner?" Leah asked.

"Or Vick, how about him? He'll be at the wedding," Celeste said.

Leah looked down at her suede ankle boots and said, "I think I might have thrown up in front of him."

"I'm sure he doesn't care."

Leah shrugged. "Well, I need to get going, but thanks for letting me see your place. It's super cute."

"No problem. I'll see you at the wedding." Celeste moved towards the door to exit Leah out.

"Yes, you will. I know Jill picked out really expensive bride's maids dresses just to stick it to me, so I had mine altered. Now Jill won't be the only one getting attention on the big day," she said, giving a devilish grin.

Chapter Nine

House Hunting

The End of March 2018

The weekend following Jill's wedding shower, Traci and Celeste went looking at a few alternative places for Celeste. Traci picked Celeste up in her SUV, coffee in hand. "You got an offer on your place this morning," Traci said, smiling a gentle smile at Celeste. "It came in a little below asking. You'll have to respond within a few days," Traci explained.

They traveled towards Malmark, a city much closer to her work. They stopped at the first of three places. Unfortunately, Celeste did not like it. It was hard for her to even explain why to Traci. It was a perfectly fine place, just not for her. It bored her to even be there, and she couldn't picture herself living there. They headed over to the second place, and Celeste did not like that one either. It was a little pricey, and even though it came with a two-car garage, it was far from the condo unit. Celeste already had an inconvenient parking situation.

The third place they looked at was just right. Celeste fell in love with it instantly–an artist's loft. The architecture of it was unique, with high ceilings and floor to ceiling windows on the north side that let in soft warm light, angel light. The townhouse had hardwood floors, a cozy fireplace, one wall entirely lined with beautiful terracotta brick, and newly remodeled bathrooms and kitchen. A Brady Bunch style floating staircase got you from the first floor up to the loft. A picturesque stream ran through the center of the complex, surrounded by tall trees. It felt very tranquil to Celeste, and the best part, it came with a two-car garage right by the unit. If it was possible to be in love with a piece of real estate, Celeste just fell in love.

"I want to make an offer," Celeste said as they left.

"Are you sure you don't want to think about it for a bit?" Traci asked.

Celeste knew how fast real estate sold in California. "No, I don't want to wait. I want to put in an offer at the asking price. I don't want to mess around by lowballing them," Celeste said. Traci put in the offer as soon as she got home from dropping Celeste off.

When Celeste got back to her place, she stared out the window at her view. She felt a twinge of sadness knowing she would miss this place, but she knew she needed to move on. After seeing the townhouse at Forest Creek, she was even more resolved than before. She prayed the seller accepted her offer. As she was deep in thought, she heard her phone bing. A text from Maybel read: **How did the house hunting go?**

Celeste texted back: **I am putting in an offer on one I saw today.**

A few minutes later, Maybel knocked at Celeste's door with a foiled plate in her hand. "Tell me all about the place, dear," she said, handing the plate to Celeste.

Celeste peeked under the foil and was not sure of what she saw. "Gluten-free blondies," Maybel said. "I baked some for Jeffrey and Jill, but Jill didn't want any. She said she no longer eats blond sugar."

Celeste laughed. "Her loss is my gain." They sat down on Celeste's couch, and the sun was setting on the city. Celeste held the plate of blondies on her lap, took one, and put her feet up on her coffee table. She offered one to Maybel, and Maybel took one and put her feet up. They munched and chatted for a long time. Celeste felt the preciousness of her time with Maybel, who really felt like a mother to her. "Did I tell you that Leah had stopped by to see my place?"

"No," Maybel said, turning her head towards Celeste in surprise.

"Yeah, and it's obvious to me she's still in love with Jeff," Celeste said. "She also said Jill is a psycho. I feel like I shouldn't tell you she said that, but if it was me, I'd want to know something like that."

"I'm glad you told me, and you're right. I need to know. Jeffrey told me him and Jill got into a horrible fight the other day. He said she was freaking out about everything and having a meltdown. I think they were fighting about money. He said it scared him." Maybel grabbed another blondie.

"Bridezilla?" Celeste asked, eating her second blondie. It tasted sweet and buttery, but there was also another distinct flavor she couldn't place.

"Who knows? I hope everything will be ok. I'm bringing shrimp cocktail as the appetizer for the wedding. I'd hate to waste money on all that good shrimp if this marriage doesn't turn out," Maybel said, laughing.

"I heard Vick got an invitation," Celeste said, giggling for some reason she wasn't sure of.

"Yeah, I told you I'm trying to be nicer to him. You know what that asshole did? He tried to *fine* me for the booze at the wedding shower!" Maybel huffed.

"Can he do that?" Celeste asked, still giggling.

"No, he can't! He's just drunk with power! I reminded him of the bylaws under our homeowners' association. As you might recall, years ago, I had been the president of the co-op board before we converted to condos. I helped write the bylaws, and I know those rules inside and out. I know them better than that idiot any day of the week. Besides, he has no proof I brought the alcohol, which I didn't."

"Did you know Leah was going to bring alcohol?"

"Don't worry about that, dear."

Celeste laughed again. "I heard Leah threw up in her car on the way home."

"Yeah, Vick told me that when I asked him how it went. He said it just sort of sprayed out everywhere, and garbanzo beans got stuck in the gearshift," Maybel said.

"I was surprised she drank the wine you gave out as a prize. Leah looks like the type that would turn her nose up at it."

"Oh please! That girl would put any drink in her mouth," Maybel said, chuckling. "You know what? I think there's weed in these blondies."

"Where did you get weed?"

"Don't worry about that. It's medicinal for my arthritis… but I think I grabbed the wrong butter out of the fridge," Maybel said, blinking and running her tongue along her teeth. "I think my teeth are growing."

"Well, this explains why I can't stop laughing," Celeste said. She looked out her window, stopped laughing, and gazed at the view. It felt like the first time she'd seen it. The depth of the city overwhelmed her. She imagined falling out of her window.

"Dear, are you hungry? I have some leftover chicken cutlets and fettuccine at my place," Maybel offered.

"Let's go." Celeste and Maybel exited her place and went to Maybel's.

Jeffrey Morgan's handsome face stared back at Celeste as she looked at a family photo hanging on Maybel's wall. He was much younger, at least 15 years younger in the picture. Maybel's hair in the photo made her look like Gina Lollobrigida. Her husband George stood next to her, looking like a proud man.

Celeste could see where Jeffrey got his good looks, a perfect blend of both parents.

Maybel said about George, "I miss him."

"I know," Celeste replied, fighting back tears. She felt her own grief for her own family. They sat down at Maybel's Formica table and ate cold chicken cutlets. "God, this is good." The food tasted delicious. The oregano Maybel added to the breadcrumbs coating the chicken danced on her tongue.

"I hope Jeffrey doesn't quit the fire department. He's always loved his job." Maybel twirled some pasta around her fork.

"What would he do for Jill's dad's company?" Celeste grabbed an apple from the fruit bowl on Maybel's table. It made the most beautiful crunching sound when she bit into it. What a sweet crisp apple, she thought. As the juice from the flesh of the apple dazzled her taste buds, she knew why they made apple juice from apples.

"I don't really know. I don't think Jeffrey knows either." Maybel got up and got a box of crackers out of her cabinet. When she bit into the buttery Ritz cracker, the chunk she took out of it left the cracker looking like a crescent moon. Maybel stared at it for a second before popping the rest of it into her mouth.

The apple distracted Celeste, and she said, "You know, I don't have a lot of memories of my mom because she passed away when I was so young, but I do remember her making me French toast. She'd spread peanut butter on it and top it with applesauce. It was my favorite breakfast. Sometimes, she'd even put a thin layer of sour cream on it. I remember how good it was."

Eventually, Maybel and Celeste moved to Maybel's tiny cozy den because Celeste wanted to play some 45s. Maybel and George had one of the best collections of vinyl records

Celeste ever saw. Somewhere between listening about Elvis's suspicious mind and Chuck Berry having no particular place to go, Celeste pulled out the *Yackety Yak* single. She held it up and showed Maybel, who nodded approval, remembering how George always got a kick out of that song.

When the song ended, Maybel said, "George was so proud of Jeffrey when he became a firefighter. He raised Jeffrey to be a good, responsible man. I wish he were here to see him get married." Maybel wiped a tear from her eye. Celeste's heart broke for her.

Celeste sat on the floor looking at Maybel sitting on her loveseat in the dimly lit den and saw the melancholy on Maybel's face, a half-eaten melting bowl of Neapolitan ice cream on the coffee table in front of her. "I can imagine," Celeste said, putting down the jar of peanut butter she'd been holding and moved over to the loveseat next to Maybel. She noticed a beautiful afghan resting on the back of the couch she hadn't seen before. "Is this new?" Celeste wondered.

"I knitted it for Jeffrey and Jill as a wedding gift, but when I told Jill about it, she said she's allergic to yarn," Maybel said, throwing her head back, laughing.

Celeste looked closer at the lovingly handmade knitted blanket with an intricate pattern woven into the beautiful wool. She made a delightful blend of purple, blue, green, and teal. The peacock colors, Celeste thought, and she knew how hard Maybel tried. Feeling very sleepy, Celeste curled up on the loveseat next to Maybel and dozed off. Later, Maybel covered Celeste with Celeste's new peacock colored blanket.

Chapter Ten

Shrimp Fest

April 21, 2018, Pre-nuptials

From behind anti-glare wrap-around sunglasses with 100% UVA/UVB protection, Maybel watched Celeste place a huge box in the trunk of her car. "Be careful with that shrimp, dear." After loading up everything for the shrimp cocktail appetizer for Jeffrey and Jill's wedding, they got on their way down to the dock.

Celeste wore an aqua blue dress that looked lovely on her, and she paired it with a black belt that emphasized her hourglass waist. She pulled her long dark hair back into a messy bun at the nape of her neck, sticking the turquoise beaded hair comb in the side of her knotted bun. The choker with cameo embraced her neck snuggly. When she walked, she could feel the thin, cold metal chain slide around from her neck down her back.

Maybel's ankle length forest green dress with three-quarter sleeves and a square neckline covered her body in an age-appropriate manner. The gigantic beaded peacock necklace perched heavily on her décolleté, while the feathered barrette stuck straight up on the side of her head. She felt and looked ridiculous.

When they got to the boat, Celeste stood for a minute, looking at it. The bright white multi-level vessel glistened in the sunlight on that perfectly warm breezy California day - **Knot Your Nuptials** printed on the side of it in nautical navy-blue script. As she breathed in the salt air and watched the seagulls fly around, she told herself it should be perfectly safe, right? She took a deep breath and followed Maybel up the ramp. Maybel carried two bags of ice, while the box Celeste carried held the shrimp, Maybel's silver serving bowl, tiny plastic cups, a pint of homemade cocktail sauce with horseradish and a couple of plastic bags of lemon wedges. A young man from the boat's crew named Christopher escorted them to the deck to a table set up for it. Celeste helped Maybel set everything out but refused to handle the shrimp. "I don't want to smell like shrimp," she said.

"That's fine, dear. Will you start putting cocktail sauce in the little cups, and each one gets a lemon wedge on the side," she instructed.

They worked quietly side by side for a little while. Maybel placed the shrimp on the bed of ice that she poured into her giant silver serving bowl, arranging them in neat concentric circles. Celeste admired how Maybel loved her son. She didn't buy bags of frozen shrimp like most people would. She bought several pounds of fresh shrimp, cleaned and cooked them herself. These little things were acts of love for her. Once Maybel finished putting the tiny pink crustations on the ice, she excused herself to wash her hands again.

Guests would arrive around 5 PM. The boat's crew rushed around, setting out the chairs on the main deck for the wedding ceremony. Others were inside the enclosed area of the main deck, setting up the dining tables. The caterer put out guacamole and blue corn chips next to the shrimp cocktail. Maybel wasn't sure that really went with her appetizer, but Jill had insisted on a vegan option.

Diane came up from below deck where Jill's makeshift dressing room was located and looked frantic in an exquisitely tailored periwinkle suit. When Maybel asked Jill's mother if everything was alright, she explained, "Jill's bridesmaids still aren't here. They're running late, and Jill is getting stressed out."

"Maybe we can help," Maybel offered. "Does she need any assistance with anything?"

"No, she's all ready to go. She just needs to stay calm," Diane said.

Celeste noticed Diane wore a beautiful amethyst and purple jade broach. The plum-colored stones glistened in the sun. She wondered if Jill designed it, but when she asked, she was told it was one of Leah's designs. Clearly, Leah's designs were better than Jill's, Celeste thought.

Maybel asked, "Does Jill have her something old, something new, something borrowed and something blue?"

Diane nodded. "Yes, her dress is new. There are blue flowers mixed with her bouquet. She's wearing an old pair of my designer heels, and I think she's borrowing a piece of jewelry from Leah."

"Mom!" Jeffrey shouted, walking up behind Maybel. He gave her a big bear hug, and Celeste suspected he'd already started drinking. His groomsmen, Eddie, and Danny were with him and were just as boisterous. They were all dressed in dark teal tailored suits with white dress shirts and various peacock-colored ties. Jeff's childhood friends seemed very familiar with Maybel and clearly loved her and her invitations to lasagna dinners over the years. Celeste snapped some photos of all of them with Maybel. The joyful moment captured in their smiles, and the beautiful vast ocean behind them.

Guests started arriving on the boat, gathering on the main deck. Celeste really didn't know anyone who arrived at that point. She walked away by herself and stood for a while at the railing of the boat, looking out at the water. She breathed in the briny air. Even though she could not see them, she knew the sharks were lurking out there.

Around that time, Detective Brian Bahn landed on the boat. He got himself an appetizer, then walked around searching for Celeste. He spotted her at the edge of the deck. He stood and gazed at her for a minute, noticing the little chain dangling down her back. He wanted to pull on it. "Fancy meeting you here," he said, circling around behind her.

She turned to see him wearing a teal dress shirt, tucked in, and black slacks. She smiled.

Brian reached for her hand. "I knew that was you. I recognized you from behind."

"I don't know if I should be flattered or insulted." His hand was so warm.

"Flattered." Brian let go of her hand and ran his hand through his hair. Celeste noticed he hadn't gotten it cut in a while, and he'd grown out his sideburns an inch.

"Is that a new shirt?" Celeste asked.

"Yeah, I asked the saleslady if they had any teal shirts," he said, holding out his arms, a cup of shrimp cocktail in one of his hands. "I've never seen this color before."

"You look good in that color. It brings out the depth in your eyes."

He looked at her and noticed her crimson-colored lips, another color he felt like he hadn't seen before. They shimmered in the sunlight. To get a kiss from those ruby lips would be a treasure, he thought. He asked about her phobia. "We're finally here on the boat. Are you feeling alright?"

"We haven't set sail yet." She looked back out at the water and crossed her arms against the railing, resting on it.

Brian dangled a shrimp covered in cocktail sauce over the railing. "I could throw some bait in the water to see if there are any sharks out there."

Celeste quickly slapped his hand back. "Stop it! That's not funny! And don't waste good shrimp. Maybel won't like that," she warned, but a laugh escaped her pretty red lips.

He popped the shrimp, sans the tail, in his mouth. "Man, this cocktail sauce has a kick to it!"

"That's from the horseradish Maybel puts in it," Celeste said. "It's like an atomic bomb exploding on your tongue."

"You know, with the way you're dressed, you kind of look like Betty Rubble," Brian observed, looking her up and down.

Celeste thought about her aqua blue outfit with black choker and dark hair and felt embarrassed. "Oh geez! I didn't even realize…"

"If you'd like, I can be your Barney. I'd just have to take my pants and shoes off and put on an animal pelt."

Laughing, she blushed and looked away. "Maybe later."

Brian raised his eyes brows at her. Perhaps the iceberg was melting. Chicks always feel romantic at weddings, he thought, calculating his odds of getting lucky. But he knew she needed baby steps.

"Jill made jewelry for all of us. She gave me this choker and hair comb, so I had to wear it," Celeste said, changing the subject. "And she said she's wearing a necklace that has two J's on it for Jill and Jeffrey."

"You think she could make a C B necklace?" he asked.

"C B? Corny Brian? Crazy Brian? Cute Brian?" Celeste asked.

"Celeste and Brian." He smiled and tilted his head.

"Oh. Or how about BC? Wait, no, that's like the measurement of time," she said. "I'm glad you got the day off." She looked at him and thought of her last relationship. What an addictive love affair it was and riddled with his deceit. She wondered what Brian's deceit would be, but for the moment, she was enjoying her time with him.

"Me too. I've been working a lot of hours lately. This is my first day off in two weeks." He moved closer to her, leaning on the railing and mirroring her body language. He kissed her cheek and said, "Your hair smells like coconut."

"You smell like cocktail sauce."

The crowd on the boat grew loud with laughter and conversation. There were about one hundred people on the boat. When she looked through the crowd, Celeste saw Leah and Kristen board the ship carrying gifts. They quickly went below deck to Jill's dressing room. She got a glimpse of Leah's backless dress, and the front of it barely covered her lady area in the shiny shade of electric purple fabric. Kristen wore a more tasteful knee length teal dress with spaghetti straps.

Maybel stomped past Brian and Celeste, looking annoyed. She uttered, "That numbskull dropped shrimp all over the deck! I told him not to waste good shrimp!"

"Who was she talking about?" Brian asked Celeste after Maybel walked past them.

"Vick," Celeste answered, "has to be Vick." She spotted her friend Veronica, her date Tom, and Vick, over by the shrimp cocktail. "Let's go mingle," she said, leading the way. He watched her walk in front of him, and he could barely wait to get a hold of her.

"Celeste! You look beautiful!" Veronica reached out to hug her long-time friend. A purple and pink floral dress flowed from her figure demurely. A French twist swept up her golden blond hair, and light pink lipstick colored her lips. When she smiled, her entire face lit up.

"You remember Brian, right?" Celeste turned and motioned to her date.

"Yes, of course. The avocado from last year's Halloween party!" Veronica reached out and shook Brian's hand.

"The alligator! Us greenies have to stick together," Brain said, shaking her hand.

Vick stood the tallest next to all of them in a green oxford. The buttons on his shirt were stretched to the limit across his potbelly, and it looked like his shirt wanted to scream at him. He asked Brian, "Did you get a look at Leah? She looks so supple."

The turning of Vick's head in the direction where he spotted Leah put his face in the sun. His eyeglasses dimmed, making him look creepier than usual. Celeste noticed he wore the kind of eyeglasses that doubled as sunglasses. Only dirty old men wear that type of glasses, she thought.

Tom, in a royal blue golf shirt and khaki pants, said, "I heard there is a peacock theme, and I saw Maybel. She's really taking the theme seriously, isn't she?"

Wanting to talk to Leah, Vick said to the group, "Excuse me. I'm going to go see if Leah needs help with anything *below deck*... if you know what I mean." He winked and disappeared into the crowd.

The boat's crew started to wrangle all the guests to take their seats for the ceremony. Celeste worked her way through the crowd on the deck with Brian hot on her heels. She found Maybel towards the front of the rows of seats. At Maybel's request, Celeste sat down next to her. Celeste whispered to Maybel, "Brian said I look like Betty Rubble from *The Flintstones*, and I'm afraid he's right."

"At least you don't have a damn peacock spread out over your chest! I swear this thing weighs like three pounds! I think it's going to puncture one of my lungs." Maybel tugged at the giant uncomfortable metal framed piece of jewelry nesting on her chest, the feathers from the clip in her hair flopping around as she did so.

Celeste suggested, "Maybe you should stop moving around. I think that's just making it worse."

"Did you see the cake!?" Maybel asked.

"No, why?"

Maybel looked mortified. "It's a three-tiered wedding cake with two peacocks–a colorful one and a white one sitting side by side. The tails fan out down the tiers, and there are cupcakes all around the bottom of it with the eye of the peacock design on the tops of each cupcake. It's really elegant, but I'm afraid because of the accessories Jill made me wear, people will think I tried to match the cake! *The cake*! And she asked me to pass out the cupcakes later. I swear she did this just to embarrass me!"

Brian sat down next to Celeste, resting his arm around the back of Celeste's chair. With a devilish grin, he tugged lightly on the little chain dangling down her back.

Jeffrey and his groomsmen walked to the front of the deck and lined up next to the minister. A lovely flowered trellis stood at the front of the deck, where the ceremony would take place. They sailed away from the harbor. Celeste realized it was anchors away. The sun was setting behind the deep blue sea. The music played, and there was no turning back now…

Chapter Eleven

Tying the Knot

April 21, 2018,
below deck minutes before the nuptials

"That's not the dress we agreed on!" Jill's tanning booth tanned skinned turned redder than a red delicious apple.

Leah smirked. "I know. It's better." The vibrant purple colored fabric barley covering her tall thin body served as no more than a handkerchief. Purple rose petal earrings dangled around the sides of her neck, and the matching rose barrette was clipped into her long, dark hair.

Jill asked, "And why are you wearing Kristen's jewelry?!"

"We're all borrowing jewelry today. Look, I brought one of my elegantly designed bracelets for you to wear on your big day, so you have your something borrowed." Leah smiled and motioned to Kristen, who had Leah's silver lip ring circled around her much less plump bottom lip. "And Kristen finally got her lip pierced. We went the other day and got it done, and the lip ring you gave me wasn't quite big enough to go around my bottom lip. You didn't size it right, Jill. But it looks great on Kristen! Besides, the purple rose petal earrings would have clashed with her teal dress. They match my purple dress perfectly." Leah smiled a smile that didn't quite reach her eyes.

Jill ordered, "Switch back with her right now!"

Leah protested, "That hardly seems sanitary at this point. Besides, what's the big deal, Jill?"

Jill's mom Diane entered the below deck dressing room and said quickly, "Jill, honey, the ceremony is ready to begin. The music has started. It's time to go!"

Leah shrugged off Jill's request. "See, there's no time." Leah walked above to the main deck, breezing past Vick, who practically drooled on her.

Kristen looked at Jill. "I'm sorry, Jill. I didn't mean to upset you. I love the lip ring and Leah said it didn't fit her lip and also, I felt weird about wearing the purple rose jewelry because of my past history with Jeff."

Jill straightened out her designer wedding gown and snapped on the bracelet Leah brought. "The purple roses don't mean anything now. Jeff is marrying me, not you! The lip ring wasn't for you. It's not your style. You look silly wearing it. You should take it off. And where is the tongue ring?"

"Jill, honey, it's time to *go*! Your father is waiting to walk you down the aisle," her mother ordered, grabbing Jill's arm leading her above deck. Kristen hurried up to the main deck ahead of them.

The nuptials

Jeffrey Morgan stood at the bow of the boat, nervous and tipsy. He thought a few drinks would calm his nerves. They did not.

Jill stood at the back of the deck with her dad's arm hooked through her arm. He could feel her shaking. Last-minute wedding jitters, Jack Jenson thought, remembering his own wedding to his beautiful bride, who bore him a beautiful daughter. Years of marriage made Diane grow bitter, but that was normal, right? Sacrifices needed to be made for the family empire, and Diane lovingly made them for him. Jack felt like a lucky man.

The two bridesmaids slowly marched down the aisle first. Kristen, bouquet in hand, made her way towards the trellis, looking like the friend any girl could tell a secret to at a slumber party. When Jeff watched Kristen march up the aisle, he wondered what she would look like in a wedding dress.

Leah followed behind Kristen but before Jill, just like in life. She clopped down the aisle, putting one lanky leg in front of the other, prancing like a show horse. Vick eyed Leah from one of the back rows while she approached the trellis. Making eye contact with Jeffrey, Leah smiled at him. She wondered what it would be like to exchange vows with him.

Jill opted for a sleeveless, A-line gown with embroidered macrame lace over organza. It looked quite couture. Her hair was piled high on top of her head while the veil floated down around her beautiful face. The train swept out gloriously behind her, a gown for a princess, indeed. Her copper double J necklace complimented the champagne color of the dress. The florist fashioned a harmonious bouquet of ivory roses, purple lilacs, and rare blue morning glories. The combination of champagne and ivory looked très chic. Jill Jenson, soon to be Jill Morgan, was a stunning bride who truly belonged on the cover of a magazine.

Jill's dainty feet propped up in her mother's vintage satin high heels glided gracefully down the aisle. Jeffrey gazed at his wife to be with her proud father, arm in arm with her. All eyes turned to look at Jill. Jeffrey's heart skipped a beat. Having a lovelier bride would be impossible, he thought. Jill's dad gave her away under the flowered trellis. The sun glowing where the water met the sky, and the boat sailed outside the harbor. Everyone sat back down, and the minister began the ceremony. Jeffrey turned to face Jill. A lace veil separated the two of them.

As everyone gathered there that day, they were both scared to death, but for different reasons. The music stopped playing. Jill carefully turned to face Jeffrey; her dress was difficult to maneuver in.

Dearly beloved guests were addressed. The man and the woman stood before all of them, ready to pledge themselves to one another for as long as they live, promising fidelity, and to stay together until their last breath. The minister spoke of the definition of love. Two flesh were going to become one. The Song of Songs sang out in their hearts. Vows were recited.

Jill went first. Her voice shaky, she said, "I unite my breath to yours that our days of love may be long."

"May our paths never end. May we be only one from this day forward," Jeffrey spoke, saying the words they'd rehearsed so many times before.

Rings were exchanged. The symbolism of the rings explained.

Guests were asked to speak now or forever hold their peace. No one spoke, not even Leah. Jeffrey was told he could take this woman to be his lawfully wedded wife. The veil lifted. The California sunlight glistened on Jill's beautiful blond highlights before the kiss took place. Jeffrey moved in to put his lips on Jill's, dipping her as he did so. Everyone clapped and cheered. Some cried. The minister pronounced them to be husband and wife.

Jill felt pleased that Kristen and Leah had to watch her marry Jeff. He was all hers now. Her smile beamed from ear to ear across the horizon of her face.

Celeste looked over at Maybel, who was crying. She hoped they were tears of joy. The guests stood and continued to clap, and Jeffrey and his new bride, Jill, held hands walking down the aisle together. The bridal party followed behind them. Vick continued to eye Leah, and Leah still eyed Jeff. Celeste put her hand on Maybel's and squeezed it.

They stood on the deck for a minute in the dusky night, breathing in the ocean air. Brian put his arm around Celeste, running his thumb along her arm. She leaned into him and felt a flutter. Feeling close to him, she wished they could just stand still in time for a while. She couldn't go back to pushing him away anymore, but she wasn't ready to move forward either.

Brian thought of his own weddings, and while she enamored him, he did not want to get married again, ever. He only seemed to make a mess of things, and Celeste deserved better than a mess.

A man from the boat's crew announced to the guests they could go into the enclosed dining room for cocktails while the bridal party needed to take photos on the top deck.

Brian kissed Celeste's cheek and whispered, "Come on, Betty, let's go get you a Brontosaurus burger."

"Shut up," she said, laughing. She straightened out her aqua blue dress. The guests slowly made their way to the dining room. Brian, not able to take his eyes off Celeste, walked behind her thinking she looked like a juicy Bosc pear, but her personality felt much more like a prickly pear cactus. He wondered how she felt about marriage but didn't want to open the door to that conversation.

Chapter Twelve

Belly Up to the Bar

April 21, 2018, drinks, and dinner

The boat's crew set up the buffet, and the bar opened with music playing softly in the background. Assigned seating sat Celeste at Maybel's table along with Brian, Vick, her friend Veronica, and her date, Tom. The bridal party would dine at a long table in the front of the room, facing all the round tables of guests.

Maybel, along with many other guests, made a beeline for the bar. The line looked too long for Celeste, who figured she would get a drink later. They mingled and chatted for a while before taking their seats.

"What a lovely ceremony!" Veronica said, smiling at everyone seated at the table.

"Yep, it's anchors away for those two," Tom added. He'd been dating Veronica for six months and was contemplating marriage with her.

"More like drop anchor," Brian mumbled under his breath. Celeste pretended not to hear him. A basket of bread in the middle of the table called to Brian, and he grabbed for it, taking his roll, and passing the basket along.

"Jeff is going to have a hot night tonight," Vick said, chewing on his pumpernickel slice. He looked at everyone sitting at the table and asked, "Do you think Jeff will take command of the bedroom?"

Maybel, back from the bar with free-flowing free drinks in each hand, scolded him, "Geez, Vick! That's my son and daughter-in-law you're talking about." She scowled at him and guzzled one of her Harvey Wallbangers.

Vick defended himself, "Well, we were all picturing the honeymoon in our heads."

Veronica thought Vick's comment was gross. She insisted, "No, we weren't!"

"We are now," Brian said, and Tom laughed.

Vick went on, "I'm just saying it's a natural thing between a man and a woman. I mean, he's either going to take command *of* the bedroom, or receive command *in* the bedroom. They have urgent needs and urges, and they should act on those urges whenever they want. And I think it's also natural for us to think about their urges and picture it."

Maybel rebuked him, "Vick! Stop fantasizing about my son on his wedding day! This is not what I invited you for!" She wondered why she had invited him. "You're an adult man and you need to behave yourself. If you keep talking like that, I'm going to report you to the captain and I'm going to tell him there is a pervert on this sailboat!"

"You know who could raise the sail on my boat?" Vick winked at the table and said, "Leah! She has the body of an agile ballerina. There're sparks of electricity just dancing off her."

Celeste shook her head. "This isn't a… we're not on a *sailboat*." She turned to Brian. "Maybel said there's a full open bar. I'm going to go get a drink. Do you want me to see if they'll make you something like a banana daiquiri with a coconut milk blast and some raspberry sprinkles on top?"

"If you're trying to get me drunk so you can take advantage of me, I'll gladly oblige," Brian said, "and for your information, they don't always put coconut milk in banana daiquiris. They put coconut milk in pina coladas."

"You want a pina colada, don't you?"

"I think you already know the answer to that," Brian replied, standing up.

Celeste stood up. "OK, let's go."

Maybel warned, "Whatever you get, don't get anything with fresh citrus. That bartender could barely pull the lever on his own juicer." She sucked the last of her Harvey Wallbanger out of the thin black straw. She looked at Veronica and said, "As the saying goes, 'The juice wasn't worth the squeeze', if you know what I mean."

"Celeste," Veronica asked, "will you see if they can make me one of those Shark Bite cocktails? You know, the one with the blue Curacao."

Celeste nodded and made her way, weaving through the tables, with Brian's hand on the small of her back guiding her as they went. They got to the end of the drink line and waited with everyone else. "Boy, did Jeff and Jill look nervous," Brian said.

"Big decision. Does attending a wedding remind you of your own weddings?" Celeste asked, stressing the S in weddings.

He smiled at her. "That is ancient history. Also, this is a happy day, so let's talk about me another time."

Celeste wondered what she was doing with him. Where could it go?

"There's a crescent moon out tonight," Brian said, pointing out the window. Nightfall was upon them. Venus twinkled next to the slivered moon shining high above the ocean rays glimmering off the ocean water. He held her hand, and she relaxed a bit.

The same man who wrangled everyone into the dining room stood by the wedding party's table with a microphone, eager to make an announcement. They cut the music. He cleared his throat. "Ladies and gentlemen, it is my honor and pleasure to announce to you for the first time Mr. and Mrs. Jeffrey Morgan!"

The guests clapped, cheered, whooped, hollered, and whistled while Jill and Jeffrey walked into the room with the wedding party trailing behind them. A soulful song from the 70s inviting you to *Come and Get Your Love* played as husband and wife smiled, waving to their guests. Kristen fumbled around a little with the train of Jill's dress, while Leah stood and watched. Leah's dress being short enough that if she had bent over, it would have been obscene.

The music made Brian think again about the dance with Celeste he missed at the Halloween party. Tonight, he would get that dance a slow one, he hoped. They finally got to the front of the drink line, and Celeste ordered a glass of white wine and a Shark Bite cocktail. Brian requested a pina colada. Making their way back to their table, they ran into Kristen. Celeste introduced Brian to her, who put his chunk of pineapple back into his drink so he could shake her hand. "Nice to meet you," he smiled, getting pineapple juice on Kristen's hand.

"You look lovely," Celeste complimented her.

"Thank you! So do you," Kristen said, coughing into her hand and rubbing her head.

"Are you getting sick?" Celeste asked.

"I don't know. I feel a little woozy. Probably just seasick, or maybe I'm a little tipsy. Leah brought a bottle of Jägermeister with her, and we did a few shots before we boarded the boat. It's strong stuff… tastes like medicine. I normally don't drink cheap stuff. I like the top shelf brands. I'm going to see if the bartender will make me a Cadillac margarita," she said, coughing again.

"Lovely ceremony. Is your family here too? I know you've known Jill for years," Celeste said.

Kristen gushed, "If I ever get married, I think I'll want to do it on a boat just like this! And no, my parents couldn't make it. They went on another European vacation. I'm sure they sent an expensive gift to Jill and Jeff, though. That's their style."

"I bet the photos you all took at sunset will be really nice," Celeste said.

"I guess so. Jill seemed kind of uptight. I guess the case of Bridezilla lasts all the way through the wedding," Kristen said with a lighthearted laugh.

"And after," Brian muttered under his breath.

"You got your lip pierced recently?" Celeste asked.

"Yeah! I always wanted to, and last week Leah took me to do it. We've been hanging out a lot lately, since Jill spends so much time with Jeff now. Leah got another piercing, too," Kristen said.

Brian wondered where.

"My dad wasn't happy about it when he saw it," Kristen said. "I work for him like how Jill works for her dad. He said it didn't look professional."

"I thought," Celeste began, "that Jill and Leah have their own company, not that they work for her dad."

Kristen giggled and rolled her eyes. "Jill's dad bankrolled the whole thing. They never would have been able to do it without him. Hey, since we're all dolled up, would you mind taking a selfie with me?"

Celeste handed off the Shark Bite cocktail to Brian and took her cell phone out of her purse. They stood arm in arm, smiling at the camera while Brian sipped his drink and watched. "What's your cell number? I'll text it to you."

When exchanging numbers, Jill's father, Jack, approached them, letting Kristen know it was almost time for her toast. He handed her a bubbly champagne glass.

"She seems nice," Brian said, making their way back to the table.

"Yeah, I think she's a sweetheart," Celeste agreed.

"So, earlier when you mentioned raspberry sprinkles, where can I get those?" he asked.

Celeste giggled and took her seat at their table again. "I don't know. I think I just made it up."

"It's our table's turn at the buffet," Maybel announced. One by one they got up and made their way over to the food table where warm silver chaffing dishes were lined up. They started at the end with stacks of clean white plates and ended at the end with the typical rice pilaf. Celeste opted for salmon, while Brian's hunger forced him to take salmon, steak, and chicken. Once back at their table, Maybel asked Celeste if she could take a few pictures of the wedding party. Celeste got her phone back out and snapped a few shots.

"OMG, *we* should take a selfie!" Brian teased. Celeste and Brain put their heads together, and Celeste held her cell phone up high and clicked the button. She took one with Veronica. Next, she took one of Veronica and Tom, a charming-looking couple–like bookends. After that, she snapped one of Maybel and Vick, but Maybel's smile looked weird. Maybel said she hadn't been invited to the top deck photo session. Celeste thought that was odd and cruel. It seemed to Celeste as if Jill and her family thought they were better than Maybel.

Everyone ate their dinners that were just a notch above cafeteria food. After the meal, Maybel sent Vick to the bar to get her another drink, and he was all too happy to oblige since he spotted Leah by the bar. When he offered to buy Leah a drink, she sneered at him, saying, "It's an *open* bar."

"Yeah, I'm open to anything. Let's see where the night goes." He winked at her. "That's a nice dress you're wearing."

"How tall are you?" she asked, looking up.

"6 foot 4 inches," he replied, lying about the last inch. He loved adding an extra inch. "You might not remember this, but the first time I met you, I drove you home."

"Oh, yeah," Leah said, "you're the one that covered me with a blanket."

"Yeah, I didn't want you to get cold. You puked everywhere in your car. It even got on my arm." He laughed, holding out his ape like arm.

"That was sweet of you to cover me up," she said, softening.

"Well… sweet is my middle name," Vick replied.

Servers cleared plates, and Kristen stood up to make her toast. They cut the music and gave her the microphone. She held her glass in the other hand. She coughed a little again, and Celeste noticed she wasn't looking good. Celeste took out her phone to catch a quick video of the toast.

"Hello everyone. I just wanted to say a quick toast to the newlyweds. Jeff and Jill, I hope you two have a lifetime of happiness! You are both amazing people, and I'm so glad you two found each other!" She paused from speaking to cough again. "Everyone, please raise your glasses to Mr. & Mrs. Morgan! Two of the finest people I know! Cheers!" Kristen chugged her drink. "Bottoms up!"

There were cheers all around, including from Maybel, who was on her third Harvey Wallbanger.

Kristen gave hugs to Jeff and Jill. Celeste stopped recording and wondered if Kristen was nervous or embarrassed because her face was turning red. Even her chest was blotchy. She handed the microphone back to the director of events, dropping it just short of his grasp. An ear-piercing screech rang out of the speakers when the microphone dropped. Kristen winced and grabbed her stomach, keeling forward. The man tried to catch her, but she went down fast. Jill jumped up and rushed to her. They couldn't be seen from where they were behind the table. Celeste heard Jill calling Kristen's name… the horror in Jill's voice was unmistakable… until silence rolled in like an eerie fog. Jeffrey sat frozen in his seat, drunk.

Leah, Jack, and Diane jumped up and moved towards Kristen and Jill. Some guests got up from their seats, making their way over to see if Kristen was OK. Jill continued to scream in a panic. "Kristen! Come on! Wake up!"

Brian jumped up, ran towards the wedding party table, did a single Kong vault over it, and pushed his way through the crowd to get to Kristen. Vick and Tom hurried around the side of the table, right behind him. Celeste sat motionless, looking at Maybel. Maybel, unsure what to do, stared at Celeste. The director of events radioed for help. Celeste thought she heard Jill sobbing. What the hell was happening?

When Brian saw Kristen's blue face and lifeless body, it clearly indicated she couldn't breathe. Jill cried over her, shaking her. Brian moved Jill out of the way and started performing CPR. He tried and tried, but it was no use. Soon the boat's medic arrived. His efforts were also no use.

Jill stood with Jeffrey now at her side. Tears rolled down her cheeks, leaving black streaks of mascara running down her pretty face. Jeffrey looked horrified. Eddie and Danny looked confused. Shocked, Leah held her hands over her mouth. Jack embraced his wife Diane, who was crying hysterically.

Everything went quiet in Celeste's mind. Her body froze as chaos swirled around her. She saw Veronica speaking to her but couldn't hear the words. Anxiety and fear coursed through her veins. Celeste heard her heartbeat pounding in her ears. An image of the murderer who tried to attack her months earlier flashed in her mind like lightning. She shook her head to shake the thought out of it and to shake herself out of what was going on, but she knew... she knew the life had exited Kristen's body. She could feel in her soul that Kristen was gone from this earth. She breathed a prayer.

Chapter Thirteen

A Line Up of Suspects

April 21, 2018, moments after Kristen's death

Through all the noise and hysterics, Celeste didn't hear anything. She forgot where she was. In a daze, she stood up, walked over to Maybel, and put her hand on Maybel's shoulder. Maybel sat still with her hands on her heart, crying. What a horrible thing to happen on a day that should have been joyful, she thought.

Feeling like she was drowning in fear, Celeste looked up to see Brian giving orders to Tom and Vick. He indicated for them to do crowd control. He rushed back around the wedding party's table and made his way through the commotion to her. "Celeste? Are you OK?" he asked. His voice sounded muffled to her.

Celeste looked at him, frowning as she thought, I am supposed to say yes… say yes, so he thinks you're ok. Celeste nodded, fighting back tears.

"Maybel, please get up and follow me," Brian ordered. He grabbed Celeste's hand and motioned to Veronica, too. He led the three of them to a bench along the side of the dining room, in front of a row of windows that looked out to the ocean. "All of you sit here, stay together, and don't eat or drink anything else. Don't touch anything either," he commanded before disappearing back into the crowd.

Maybel sat between Celeste and Veronica. Celeste put her arm around Maybel but wasn't sure if she was comforting Maybel or herself. Veronica held Maybel's hand. "Celeste, you look cold. You're shivering. I brought a shawl. Here, take it," Veronica said, handing it to her.

Celeste let go of Maybel and wrapped the piece of knitted warm fabric around herself. Maybe I'm in shock, she thought, noticing her hands were shaking. She couldn't make her hands stop shaking. "I feel like I'm going to throw up."

"Join the club," Maybel replied.

Detective Brian Bahn's day off just got canceled, and there went his dance with Celeste. Celeste watched him order people back to their seats and speak with the boat's crew, who were instructed to make a ship to shore call. After the conversation, the director of events made an announcement, giving the guests the same instructions Brian gave to Celeste, Maybel, and Veronica. He then moved to Tom and Vick, having a conversation with them, pointing to his right and to his left. After that, Tom went and stood guard at the stairwell that led down to the main deck. Tom, having been a military man, followed orders well. Vick, being a security guard, and always wishing he could have been a cop, knew what needed to be done. Vick went and stood guard at the door that led out to the top deck. The director of events got on his radio again, calling for the Coast Guard and the police this time.

Looking up, Maybel asked, "Oh, heaven and Jesus, how could this have happened?"

"Do you think she had a heart attack?" Veronica wondered.

"No, I don't think so. She was too young and healthy. Something was off with her. When I saw her by the bar, she said she was feeling woozy, and she was coughing," Celeste explained.

"She has an allergy to strawberries," Maybel remembered. "At Jill's shower, she didn't take a strawberry tart because of her allergy. Do you think she ate something with strawberries in it?"

"I don't think there was anything in the buffet that had strawberries," Veronica said.

"Yeah, I don't either," Celeste confirmed.

Brian approached them again. "I'm going to ask some questions to everyone in the wedding party up on the top deck," Brian said. "I need you ladies to continue to stay right here. Did any of you see anything strange since you've been on the boat?"

"No, I don't think so," Maybel answered.

"No, me either. But we were just remembering Kristen's strawberry allergy. And over by the bar how she said she was feeling woozy and coughing," Celeste added.

"OK, thanks. I didn't know about her allergy," Brian said, and left.

One by one, Detective Bahn took the members of the wedding party to the top deck to question them. He started with Jill. When asked exactly what she saw, she said, "I don't know. I just saw her grab her stomach and fall to the ground. I rushed to her side to help her."

"Did you notice anything strange about her today?" Detective Bahn asked.

"No, not at all. She was her usual sweet self. Oh, God, how could this have happened?" Jill sobbed.

Jeffrey was questioned after Jill and sobered up a lot in the wake of the events. The same questions were posed to him, with him answering, "I saw her fall down. I thought maybe she tripped on her heels." He was afraid to show too much emotion for fear of setting Jill off. He knew how jealous Jill was of his past relationship with Kristen. He stayed as stoic as he could.

Groomsmen were next. Groomsman #1 and best man, Eddie, didn't see anything at all and had been drinking since half past noon. Groomsman #2, Danny, who had also been drinking, said, "I saw that chick fall down after her toast." When asked if he saw or heard anything unusual that day, he replied, "I heard that tall chick Leah is into some kinky stuff." Detective Bahn shook his head and went to question the next person.

Leah's turn. She sat down and crossed her legs, exposing her underwear. Detective Bahn cleared his throat. She answered his question by saying, "I saw her give her lovely toast, and then she fell to the ground. I would have tried to help her, but Jill got to her first." She shook her head, wiping a tear from her eye.

"Was she acting strange today?" Detective Bahn asked, watching Leah closely.

"Nope." Leah shook her head again.

"Are you sure you didn't see or hear anything strange?" Detective Bahn prompted. The ocean's briny night air blew chilly on the top deck. The breeze blew through his hair, ocean mist hitting his face.

"No, just Jill acting like a prima donna. She was jealous of my dress. I had it altered," Leah said, running her hands down the sides of her dress and pushing her chest out. Years of experience whispered to Detective Bahn that Leah was hiding something. It was as obvious as the purple panties she wore.

Jack Jenson was questioned after Leah. He sat ramrod, impenetrable and responded, "I saw Kristen hand the microphone back to the director of events, and then she collapsed."

"Do you have any idea what could have happened to her?" Detective Bahn inquired.

"I really don't know," he replied.

Diane Jenson received her questions last, with her answer being, "I saw Kristen give her toast, and then she…" Diane's voice trailed off, and she wiped at her eyes with her elegant antique handkerchief. "Oh, God, her and Jill have been friends since they were little girls! Why did this have to happen?"

Diane's tears were real, this Detective Bahn knew. With a gentle tone of voice, he asked, "Mrs. Jenson, do you have any idea what could have caused this?"

Diane shook her head.

"I heard that Kristen had a severe allergy to strawberries. Is this true?" he asked, waiting patiently for the answer.

"Yes." Diane kept crying.

"Did she carry an EpiPen with her?" Detective Bahn asked.

"Yes," Diane answered, dabbing her tearful eyes.

"Then why didn't anyone try to go get it?" Detective Bahn asked.

A horrified look crawled over Diane's face. She stared at Detective Bahn, and more tears filled her eyes. She shook her head and sobbed, not able to believe Kristen was really gone. "I don't know…"

Chapter Fourteen

Everything Is Evidence

April 21, 2018, fresh off the boat

Celeste desperately wanted to get off the boat. She felt anxiety pumping the blood through her veins. The Coast Guard arrived along with the Sunshine Beach police and the coroner. Kristen's body was photographed and tended to. Celeste sat still with her arms wrapped around herself while she heard Maybel crying. She looked around the room, seeing the guests sitting at the tables, looking somber. The wedding party sat at the front table, looking downcast. Tom and Vick were still guarding the exits. Of all the things Celeste feared could happen while on the boat, this was not one of them. She watched Brian stay in action. After the boat docked in the harbor, he spoke with the boat captain, the Coast Guard, certain members of the crew, the coroner, and his fellow police officers.

Eventually, the guests were told they could disembark after they were all searched and gave their statements to the police officers. They were also asked to give their names and contact information to a crew member before going ashore so that all information could be added and crosschecked with the boat's manifest. Celeste and Veronica helped Maybel down the ramp, and when they got to dry land, Celeste breathed a sigh of relief.

Standing on the pier, Maybel remembered, "Oh, my silver serving bowl! It was an anniversary gift. I can't leave it behind."

"I'll take care of it," Celeste told Maybel, turning back around. She walked up the pier ramp. Brian stood at the top of it and did not smile at her when he saw her come back up. "Maybel brought her silver serving bowl on board for the shrimp cocktail and wants to get it back."

He frowned, looking annoyed. "Everything is evidence right now, Celeste."

"I have to tell Maybel she can't have her bowl back?"

"Yes. Look, I'll let them know we need to give it back to her after the investigation," he said.

"Investigation? So, you think there was foul play?" Celeste asked.

"Go home, Celeste," he instructed with a cold tone.

It was Celeste's turn to frown. "You usually tell me everything."

He could not do that this time. Standing on the ramp looking at her, he felt a sharp pain in his stomach. He winced.

"What's wrong?" Celeste asked, grabbing his arm.

He waved her off. "Just a stomach pain."

"Brian, you don't look good. Are you sure you're OK?"

He took a deep breath and shook his head. The nausea overwhelmed him. He turned away from her and spilled his guts, literally. Mediocre wedding food propelled over the ramp railing and down into the harbor ocean water below.

Celeste put her hand on his back. "Brian, I think you should go to the hospital. I think we need to be careful."

He nodded, a crushing pain in his head. Celeste ran to get a member of the crew to call an ambulance, her own cell phone in her purse with Maybel. She stayed with him until it arrived. After it left, she and Maybel drove to the hospital. This night keeps getting worse, Celeste thought.

After hours of waiting in the appropriately named waiting room, Celeste found out from a friendly nurse that Brian would be alright. She said they suspected some type of food poisoning, and they pumped his stomach. Samples had been sent to the lab. They were going to keep him overnight for observation, and since it was past visiting hours, they did not allow her to see him.

Celeste sat back down and looked around at the hospital. The bright fluorescent lights cast a glare on the stark white walls and floor, hurting her tired eyes. Maybel spoke to her. Celeste heard a tunneled sound. She felt Maybel's hand on her arm. She looked at Maybel. "Dear, are you alright?"

Celeste nodded. Maybel sat with her for a while before they got up to leave.

When they walked out, Maybel paused, taking off her huge peacock necklace. She sputtered, "I'm going to throw this damn thing in the trash! It's been nesting on me all day!"

Celeste snapped out of it. "No, wait! Hang on to it," she told Maybel.

Maybel protested, "Why? I am never wearing this ugly thing again. I don't care if it's real jade. Jill made me dress like a stupid peacock, and I didn't even get my peacock cupcake!"

"I just think we might need it," Celeste said softly, remembering what Brian said to her on the ramp. Everything was evidence. They continued to walk out to the parking lot with the hideous stringed jeweled bird in Maybel's hand, and the bright parking lot lights stinging Celeste's weary eyes. They got home that morning around 2 AM.

Celeste made sure Maybel got safely into her place before she went into her own. She unclasped her choker and set it down on the coffee table, rubbing her neck. She kicked off her heels and greeted her little birdie Birino who was perched on the top shelf of her bookcase, his favorite spot. "Hey little guy."

She changed into her pajamas, washed her make-up off, brushed her teeth, and crawled into bed, pulling the turquoise beaded hair comb out and setting it on her nightstand. While she laid there in the still of the dark early morning hours, she wondered again what the heck had happened. The image of Kristen's lifeless body being taken away stuck in her mind. She thought of Jeff and Jill. What a horrible day it turned out to be for them. Their wedding memories would forever have a black cloud over them. Celeste thought if she closed her eyes, she could shut out her memory of the evening, but it still tormented her mind's eye.

Then there was Brian… what happened to him? What made him sick? And what a man of action, she thought. Her concern for him held her sleep at bay for quite a while.

Chapter Fifteen

Chicken Soup for His Soul

April 22, 2018, the day after the wedding

Celeste awoke the next morning around 9 AM, tired, and instantly remembering the events of the wedding. Depression surrounded her. She threw on her robe and popped a pod into her coffee maker. Sipping her coffee, she checked her phone. A text from Veronica read: **Call me today when you have time. I want to make sure everyone is OK.**

Another text from Maybel read: **Let me know if you want to come over this morning for breakfast.**

Celeste finished her coffee, quickly showered, got dressed in a white peasant top, a black skirt, and strappy sandals, and headed over to Maybel's. But before she left her place, she sent Brian a text that read: **How are you feeling? Do you need a ride home from the hospital?**

"Oh, dear, come in," Maybel greeted her.

Celeste smelled bacon. She was starving, and she sat down at Maybel's yellow Formica table. Maybel set a plate of French toast and bacon in front of Celeste. Celeste fought back tears as she noticed Maybel had spread peanut butter and applesauce on her French toast.

"I spoke with Jeffrey this morning. He is so torn up, the poor thing." Maybel shook her head. "He said Jill cried all night. She is devastated, and obviously in light of what happened, they canceled their flight to Hawaii for the honeymoon."

"I can imagine. I wish we knew what happened," Celeste said. "I suppose they'll do an autopsy. That may give us some insight." She bit into her French toast, feeling transported to her childhood. She closed her eyes and chewed. Then her phone binged, and she had a text from Brian that read: **I'm feeling better. They are releasing me at noon. Vick is already on his way here to give me a ride. Thanks for the offer, though.**

"Is that Brian? Is he OK?" Maybel asked, sipping her coffee. She could see the relief on Celeste's face when she read her text.

Celeste smiled, breathing a sigh of relief. "Yes, he said he's feeling better. He said Vick is going to give him a ride home from the hospital."

Maybel asked, "Brian and Vick have really become quite the bosom lovers, haven't they?"

Celeste frowned and thought for a second, asking, "Do you mean bosom buddies?"

"Yes, that's what I said. Dear, I have some of my chicken noodle soup in the freezer. I think you should take some to Brian today. As you know, it has magical healing powers," Maybel said, chuckling. Maybel's homemade chicken noodle soup had been known to cure many ailments. "It's the broth with the chicken and vegetables, no noodles. You just heat it up on the stove, bring it to a boil, add the noodles and cook it until they are done. I'll send you with a baggie of uncooked pasta to put in it too."

"OK, I'll see if he wants some," Celeste consented.

Maybel knew he would.

Breakfast concluded, and with soup in hand, Celeste went back to her place. She called Veronica, and they chatted for a while. "Oh, Celeste, can you believe last night? That was so horrible. Are you guys all OK?" Veronica asked.

"Yes, we're OK. Maybel said Jeff and Jill had a rough night. Brian is being let out of the hospital today, and Vick is giving him a ride home."

"Oh good. Let me know if you need anything from Tom or I," she offered.

Celeste smiled. Veronica and Tom were getting along nicely, and Celeste felt happy about that. They signed off, and Celeste sent Brian another text that read: **Maybel wants me to bring you some of her chicken noodle soup.**

A half hour later, he texted back: **I don't need a nurse-maid, but if you want to wear a nurse's uniform for me.....**

Celeste laughed and texted back: **LOL Don't push your luck. You must be feeling better**.

He texted his address back to her, with her replying: **See you soon.**

After noon, Celeste made the drive down the shore and over to Brian's place. He lived on the other end of town and was not in the best neighborhood. He resided in an old one-bedroom apartment in a building built in the 1960s. The place looked more like a motel than an apartment complex. The two-story building was constructed as a square with a small pool in the middle courtyard. Celeste climbed the stone steps of the floating staircase up to the second level and heard a baby cry from somewhere, a loud television blasting out a game show, and a yapping dog.

Brian opened the door wearing plaid flannel pajama pants and no shirt. He ran a hand through his hair, and he smiled at the beautiful woman who stood at his doorstep. It felt like a dream to see her there. He wondered if the tide was turning, and she was finally rolling towards him.

Celeste could see the fatigue on his face. She stepped into his apartment, feeling relieved to see it kept clean. She noticed it had a similar layout to her place, but without the second bedroom, built-in bookcases, or the view. His view was of a back alley and another old apartment complex across the way. She could see this through the sheer curtains blowing around in the ocean breeze. The traffic hummed by outside. Alimony payments to one of his two ex-wives kept Detective Brian Bahn broke and continually paying for his sins.

"I can heat this up on the stove for you if you've got a pot I can use," she said, holding up the container of soup. He showed her where everything was in the kitchen and watched her prepare it. She looked down at the old, dingy linoleum tile in his kitchen. Describing his apartment as modest would be an understatement. Remembering Maybel always put fresh cracked pepper on it, Celeste did the same. She grabbed some party crackers she found in his cabinet. She brought everything over to him and asked him if he wanted any 7 Up. "I stopped at the store and got some for you," she said, handing him the soda.

He reached forward from the brown couch he lounged on, grabbing the green can from her hand. It tasted so good to him. His stomach was still queasy from the night before. A poster of a vintage cop car was on the wall above his sofa. She set the soup and crackers down on his glass coffee table and took a seat on a stone blue corduroy chair next to the couch. He picked up a round cracker and bit into it. He held up the cracker with the bite out of it and said, "Look, it's crescent shaped like the moon last night." With salt on his lips, he smiled at Celeste.

She smiled back and noticed a can of red spray paint on his bar next to a stack of newspapers. Who reads the newspaper nowadays? She also noticed, like her place, there were no pictures of family displayed.

He eyed her peasant top and hoop earrings. "You look like a gypsy today." Sipping his carbonated beverage, he wondered if she could tell him his fortune. She looked like she knew how to read the cards and tell everyone's deepest, darkest secrets. He rubbed the cold can across his warm, throbbing forehead.

Lifting his arm to rub the cold can on his warm brow, exposed a tattoo on the left side of his chest near his heart. It appeared to be a raven, and the raven held a rope in its mouth twisted into a noose with a heart dangling at the bottom of the rope. While Celeste didn't have any tattoos herself, she'd always thought that tattoos on the right man were quite sexy. She forced herself to stop looking at his tattoo. "Are you cold? Do you want to put a shirt on?" she asked, wondering if he always slept shirtless.

Brian grinned and said, "I thought we were going to give me a sponge bath."

Celeste squirmed.

He said, "Please tell Maybel I said thank you for the soup. That was very thoughtful of her."

"Well, we were both worried about you." Celeste rested her arms on the wooden arms of the chair but couldn't really relax.

He nodded. "Yeah, I got my stomach pumped on my day off. That was fun."

"They don't normally pump people's stomachs for food poisoning, do they, Brian?" Celeste asked.

"No, they don't, Celeste."

"What kind of poison do they think you ingested?" Celeste asked.

Brian was reluctant to answer, but not because he didn't trust Celeste. Thoughtfully, he said, "They found traces of silver cyanide… not enough to kill me, but enough to make me sick."

"Cyanide?" Celeste's eyes widened and her heart rate quickened.

"Well, silver cyanide, which is different," he explained. Celeste stared at him, silently. He went on, "We also have the preliminary results from Kristen's autopsy back because they put a rush on it. They found silver cyanide in her, too."

"Oh my God, someone poisoned her? It wasn't an allergic reaction?" Celeste asked, putting her hands in her lap leaning forward.

"They also found some sort of strawberry fluid in her stomach as well," he answered.

Celeste frowned. "Do they know which actually killed her?"

"Primarily the highly concentrated silver cyanide, but we're still unsure how that got into her body, or the strawberry liquid, for that matter. The silver cyanide might not have been enough to kill her either, but coupled with her severe allergic reaction to the strawberries, those two things did her in quickly."

Celeste felt dumbfounded. Again, she wondered, what was going on? "Last night, before you did CPR, did you suspect she'd been poisoned?"

"Yes," he said, rubbing a hand over his bare stomach.

Celeste couldn't help but notice he kept drawing attention to his torso. She took a deep, calming breath and asked, "Did you think it would be risky for you to do CPR on her?"

"I didn't have time to think. I had to act." He sipped his soda.

"Where did you learn to jump over a table like that?"

He grinned proudly at the thought of her seeing him jump. "High school track and field–long jump," he answered. "You have to have impeccable timing. Any other questions?" He was still grinning.

"Who do you think killed Kristen?"

"We don't know yet, but the investigation is under way," he responded.

Celeste tried to process all of this in her head but could not. Feeling overwhelmed again, she stood up and said, "I should go and let you get some rest. Eat your soup." She smiled and grabbed her purse.

He stood up with her and asked, "Are you sure you don't want to stay and give me that sponge bath we talked about?"

Celeste laughed. "I'm sure, but I'll give you a hug," she said, reaching out for him. They embraced in the middle of his humble apartment, shag carpet underfoot. Celeste turned her head to the side and pressed her face against his chest, and with her cheek against his raven tattoo, she heard his heart beating. He rested his cheek on the top of her head, rubbing her back. His hug soothed her, and she felt a wave of peace wash over her. She was grateful he was alive.

"You know, Celeste, all we have is right now."

"Why are you saying that to me?"

He kept his arms around her. "Because I think you need to forgive yourself for your past relationship choices, and I think you need to forgive the people that hurt you and are still holding you back. Once you do that, you can heal yourself and live in the present moment."

"Hey, I came over here to take care of you, and now you're taking care of me."

He leaned his head down and pressed his forehead against hers and said, "We can take care of each other."

Celeste closed her eyes and made a wish—a wish that made her feel like she was jumping into the deep blue sea. She knew he was right, and she knew she needed some healing. She let out a deep breath, and he felt it against his chest like a cool breeze. She felt warmth on her forehead from his forehead and asked, "Do you have a fever? You feel hot."

"That's just my normal animal musky sexual sex appeal. But yeah, I'm still running a low-grade fever."

"Eat your soup, and I'll talk to you later. Get some sleep if you can. Your body needs rest," Celeste instructed before she left.

Standing at his front window, Brian looked through his sheer curtains. He pressed the cold can of soda across his feverish forehead and watched her breeze down the steps like the ebb of the ocean, and he wondered when he'd see her again. His neighbor's wind chimes made music in a gust of wind, and he knew Celeste really was a gypsy fortune teller.

Descending the steps of the floating staircase, Celeste looked over at the aqua blue pool glimmering in the sunlight. She wondered if Brian ever swam in it. She also wondered where you get silver cyanide.

Chapter Sixteen

Slip Sliding Away

Once back from Brian's, Celeste kicked off her gold strappy sandals, slipped into her lavender sequined slippers, and poured herself a stiff drink. Honey whiskey over ice with a twist of lemon never tasted so good. Sitting down on her couch, she stared out her window. The sun would set soon, and the city lights would glitter like diamonds and pearls, but for that moment, the rays shined bright against the building windows. When there was a knock at her unlocked door, she called out, "Come in."

"Dear, how did you know it was me?" Maybel wondered.

"Just a lucky guess. Do you want a drink?" she offered, and Maybel accepted.

"So, how is Brian?" Maybel inquired.

"He seems OK. He has a low-grade fever." Brian had not specifically sworn Celeste to secrecy, and since this involved Maybel's son, she felt compelled to tell her what Brian revealed to her.

Maybel's eyes popped open wide, and she clutched her chest. "Cyanide?!"

"Silver cyanide. He said it's different, but I'm not sure what it is." Celeste sipped the last of her drink and got up to get another.

"Well, let's look it up," Maybel said, taking out her cell phone from the pocket of her black polyester pants. She brought up a search engine and typed in 'silver cyanide' with her hot pink perfectly manicured acrylic nails she got done for

Jeffrey's wedding. "It's some sort of odorless powder used in plastics, developing photographs, in electroplating, and silver plating." Maybel looked up from her phone, frowning.

"Who did Kristen know that would have access to it, or use it?"

"Dear, I think you know," Maybel replied, finishing her drink. She shook her empty glass of ice at Celeste, indicating she wanted another. "Jill and Leah make jewelry!"

"No, I think they just design and sell jewelry at Jaded Edge. I don't think they actually make it," Celeste pointed out and continued, "Jack's umbrella parent company makes it. Didn't you say his company makes plastic and metal molds and things like that?"

"Oh, that's right! They have a big manufacturing warehouse down at the dock by the harbor. Dear, I don't have a good feeling about this. Since Vick seems to have an in with Leah, maybe we can get him to obtain some intel on her," Maybel suggested.

Celeste wasn't sure if it was the two drinks of two shot honey whiskies she'd just downed, but Maybel's idea sounded great to her. "Should we go talk to him now?"

"Yes, let's go see what that tool can find out."

Another drink later, they were in the old creaky elevator descending to Vick's place on the third floor. On the way down, the alcohol gave Celeste the courage to break some news to Maybel. Celeste said, "I accepted an offer on my place. I've been meaning to tell you, my offer on the loft was accepted, too. I'm in escrow. I'll be moving out in a few weeks." Celeste had been worrying that Maybel would feel she was abandoning her. She quickly added, "But we'll still be in touch all the time, and I intend on keeping our standing Saturday lunch dates. I can either come get you, or you can order a car ride over. I'll even pay for it and Thursday night dinners we can still do too, if you want to."

"Of course, and I'm happy for you, dear. You need to go where you can find peace," Maybel said, reassuring her and meaning it.

A light that was out in the hallway on Vick's floor kept it dimly lit. "You know, you'd think the president of the HOA would take care of this dark hallway! It could be a liability if someone got hurt." Maybel and Vick's long-standing feud never ended.

"Ladies, what can I do for you?" Vick greeted them. His balding head stood just under the door frame. The view of the industrial east side of town hung like a modern art painting behind him.

Maybel began, "Vick, we need for you to do something for us. We—"

He interrupted, "Maybel, I told you, I'm not resigning as president, and you don't have the grounds to impeach me, nor do you have the votes for a recall. No one has done more for this building than I have!"

"That's not what this is about this time," she said, straightening out her black and pink floral top. "It's about Leah."

"Oh, Leah, what a sleek purebred of a woman! I tried to buy her a drink at the wedding, but she insisted that wasn't necessary," Vick said.

Maybel rolled her eyes. "Vick, it was an *open* bar. The drinks were free. Besides, she probably lost her appetite when you hit on her."

Vick looked annoyed. "You know, Maybel, everyone in this building thinks I'm a pervert and I know you had something to do with all the rumors going around—you and your phone tree!"

Averting her eyes, Maybel looked down at her orthopedic shoes.

Vick continued, "And I don't appreciate it. I'm a stand-up guy. I've done more for the residents of Regal Palms than any other HOA president, including you. I'm like a great oak of a man." He puffed out his chest proudly.

Maybel, referring to some scandalous nude photos of him she'd seen a few months prior when he engaged in a sexual entanglement with a neighbor, muttered under her breath, "Yeah, if that oak was covered in moss, hairy, *hairy* moss everywhere."

Vick's head jerked towards Maybel like a pop-up rotating lawn sprinkler head, and he spouted, "See! I knew you were telling everyone that!"

Maybel stood up as straight as she could, Vick still towering over her. She sputtered, "You brought a whole new meaning to that old joke 'love thy neighbor but don't get caught'!"

Vick looked down at her. "Maybel, what happens between two consenting adults in this building is none of your business!"

Celeste interrupted the fight and said, "Vick, we need you to gather a little intel for us."

Vick, always wishing he could have been in law enforcement and willing to do just about anything to help his good buddy Detective Bahn, looked intrigued. "I'm listening…"

Maybel explained all the information they had, and what they suspected, with Vick nodding his head. "So, you think Jill or Leah got a hold of some of the silver cyanide and poisoned Kristen? Why would they do that? I thought Kristen was like their best friend," Vick asked, rubbing his stubbly chin.

"We're not sure. Maybe they thought Jeffrey was still in love with Kristen," Maybel answered, knowing her son well.

"Something odd happened last night," Vick remembered. "Leah needed a ride home, and being the gentleman that I am, I was glad to oblige."

Maybel rolled her eyes at him again.

"Do you want to hear this or not?" Vick asked.

Maybel nodded.

Vick went on, "But before I took her home, she wanted to stop at the warehouse. You know, the one they all work at down by the dock near the harbor? So, I waited in the parking lot for her for a while, and then she came out with some papers in a blue folder."

"Did you get a look at them?" Celeste asked.

Vick shook his head.

"Do you think you could get a look at them?" Maybel asked. "Perhaps you could get together with her for a drink and console her over the loss of her friend? Maybe get her a little tipsy and find out if she knows anything?"

Celeste nodded, feeling tipsy herself. The third honey whiskey settled in, making her head fuzzy.

"Yeah, I'll get on it. I could tell last night she's totally DTF," Vick said.

When Maybel asked what DTF meant, Celeste shook her drunk head and interrupted them, pointing to Maybel and then to Vick. "No, don't ask, don't tell. Look, Vick, we just need you to question Leah about whatever paperwork she took from the warehouse last night. Do you think you can do that?"

"Sure," he answered. Moments later, Vick texted Leah, asking if she wanted to meet up.

She did.

With Vick on his way to see Leah, Maybel and Celeste hopped back in the elevator. "Dear, what is DTF?"

Celeste concentrated on the elevator buttons, found the nine, and pushed it. "It just means she wants to hook up."

"Oh. In my day, we called that hot to trot." Maybel fluffed her silver hair while looking in the mirrored wall of the elevator.

An hour later, Vick met Leah at a dive bar in town, not too far from the warehouse. Her white jeans were almost as tight as her skin, and her black blouse could be seen through. A beautiful black onyx ring on her skinny index finger accessorized her outfit perfectly. The design was all hers. They ordered cocktails and talked about how horrible the wedding was. Since Vick was buying, Leah ordered a Cadillac margarita.

"What a way for things to go down at Jeff and Jill's wedding, huh? That was some crazy boat ride. I can't believe your friend died," Vick said, shaking his head sympathetically. He reached his hand out and put it on hers, feeling the cool onyx stone beneath his finger. He felt the electricity from her.

"Yeah… tragic. Jill is so upset. Jeff can't even console her. The whole thing was so shocking. I mean, you saw Kristen when you were below deck. She was perfectly fine," Leah said. "By the way, how old are you?"

"Forty-two," Vick answered. "I know what you're going to say. I look young for my age."

"Actually, I thought you were a lot older because of your bald spot, but I got a thing for older men," Leah replied, licking some salt off the rim of her margarita glass.

Upon seeing this big lick, Vick completely forgot what he was supposed to ask Leah, and the insult she'd just hurled at him didn't land. "Let's get more drinks."

When Leah finished her second margarita, she confided in Vick, "You know, I went out with Jeff before Jill did."

"Why did you break up?" Vick asked, sipping his margarita.

Leah let out a long breath. "He dumped me when he met Jill, which is a shame because I loved him first, and I loved him more."

Several drinks and salt licks later, they ordered a car ride. The margarita goggles Leah wore were making Vick look good. They stumbled out of the Uber and docked at Leah's place. The throes of their passion made them progress from the couch to Leah's bedroom. With a powerful tug, Vick peeled off Leah's skin-tight white jeans. Leah giggled when Vick took off his shirt. She didn't think she'd ever seen a man so hairy, but the alcohol made it bearable. In fact, through her intoxication, he seemed like a great big fuzzy teddy bear.

Satin sheets adorned Leah's bed, and Vick had never operated on satin sheets before. Once they were both fully unclothed, Vick took command of the bedroom. They slip slided away all over her bedding. Leah proved to be much more limber than Vick anticipated. They rolled to the right, with limbs tangled up, and they rolled to the left and flip-flopped around. When Leah performed her signature bouncy move on Vick, who was lying prostrate on the edge of her California king-size bed, they accidentally slid right off, landing on the floor with a thud. The agony of precipitating to the ground hit Vick hard, but he rallied and finished victoriously on the floor, sailing into the ecstasy he desired. Lying on the carpet, he wondered if he tore something or popped a disk during their intense copulation.

Panting in the afterglow, Leah rested next to him. After a minute, she said, "I think I have to throw up!" She jumped up on her knees, grabbing the trash can by her bed. Vick watched her puke into it. Naked and sweaty, he hobbled back into her bed, under the cool satin sheets. When Leah was done heaving, she slipped into bed next to Vick. She moved her mouth in for a kiss, but Vick rolled his head away from her, the stench of her acidy breath not appealing to him.

Leah rested her head on her pillow and confided in Vick, "I still don't see what Jeff sees in Jill. There's nothing she has that I don't have except maybe money, but she doesn't have as much of that as people think."

Uninterested in Leah's pillow talk, Vick said, "Let's get some sleep, babe."

They both drifted off under the silky-smooth covers. A few hours later, Vick awoke to the sound of Leah's snoring. He suddenly remembered what he was supposed to do. The intel! Slowly and quietly, he slid out of her bed, and in his nakedness, began to search Leah's apartment for clues. While walking around, he felt a burning on his knee. He looked at it and realized he'd sustained a rug burn during their intercourse on the carpet.

He clicked off a few cell phone photos of some interesting documents he found in the blue folder she'd taken with her from the warehouse the night of Jeffrey and Jill's wedding. He opened her refrigerator, rummaged around, and selected a strawberry nonfat yogurt to snack on. He looked through her underwear drawer but found no clues there. With the search completed, he went into her bathroom, poked around in her medicine cabinet, put some Neosporin on his sex wound, and as the old expression goes, he 'dropped the kids off at the pool'. After using her deodorant, he got dressed and slid out the door. Leah snored the entire night through.

Chapter Seventeen

Shop 'Til You Drop

Celeste got ready for work the next morning with a slight hangover, and her head pounded harder than the rain hitting her windows. She drank a glass of water and massaged her throbbing temples. When a knock hit her front door, she jumped. The last time someone was at her door that early, they tried to kill her. Be calm, she told herself. She trudged to her door and looked out the peek hole. Maybel. "What's going on? Did Vick get some intel?"

"Based on his text to me, I think the only thing Vick got last night was lucky. His text said, '**Leah looks like an angel when she sleeps–a drunk little angel**'. And then he used the little angel emoji," Maybel went on, "but look at this." Maybel showed Celeste some pictures from her cell phone Vick sent.

Celeste zoomed in on them. "I'm not sure what I'm looking at."

"Receipts and invoices," Maybel replied.

"For turquoise?"

"And jade. Vick took these pictures last night at Leah's place when she was sleeping. He said this was what was in the blue folder she took from the warehouse."

"Why did she go to the warehouse right after the wedding, and Kirsten's death, to take payables and receivables for turquoise and jade?" Celeste wondered.

"Good question," Maybel said. "I think we need to set up a sting operation! We could even go down to the warehouse tonight and search the perimeter for more clues!"

Celeste, in the light of day and sober, objected. "No, no, no. We need to let Brian know about this. Maybe he can look into it." Celeste sent him a text asking him to call her. Remembering her own photos, she got her phone and scrolled through all the pictures she took at the wedding. She also watched the video she took of Kristen's toast. "Oh, God! Maybel, look at this!"

"What? What am I supposed to see?" Maybel asked.

"Look at the bottle on the wedding table. Does it look familiar?"

Maybel took another look, and her jaw dropped. "That looks like one of the bottles of sparkling Italian wine I gave out as a prize at the wedding shower, but Leah drank all of hers."

"It was strawberry wine! Who got the other one?" Celeste asked.

Maybel went white as a ghost and quietly replied, "Jill."

"Oh, that's right! Everyone kept talking to her about her wedding and what a beautiful bride she was going to be, and she kept taking everyone's rings," Celeste remembered.

Maybel cried, putting her hands over her heart. "Oh, God, this is all my fault! If I hadn't of given out the sparkling strawberry wine, Kristen would still be alive!"

"No, Maybel, this isn't your fault at all. You shouldn't blame yourself. It was just an accident," Celeste said. "Besides, she was poisoned, remember?"

At that moment, Brian called Celeste, and she got him up to speed on everything. He said Vick already sent him the photos of the receipts and invoices. He asked Celeste to send him the video of the toast and all her pictures from the wedding. He would obtain a search warrant for the warehouse. "Also, please tell Maybel her soup was amazing! I feel good as new today," he said before signing off.

"What did he say?" Maybel asked.

"Hang on," Celeste said, walking back to her bedroom. She returned with her turquoise hair comb. Celeste looked at it closely, asking Maybel, "What are you doing today?"

"Not much. Why?"

"How would you like to go to the jeweler with me?" Celeste asked.

"Don't you have to go to work today?"

Celeste smiled and faked a cough. "I'm feeling a little sick. I'm going to call out."

Since it was raining that day, they bundled up. Celeste dug out her stylish pink and purple plaid trench coat from the back of her closet, some black rain boots, and an umbrella with a huge pink flower on it. They headed out to a local jeweler Celeste knew - an elderly African American gentleman who looked through the wisest eyes Celeste ever saw. His curio and confectionary shop, called The Velvet Sapphire, was located over on 4th Street, and housed the most fabulous bibelots and treasures like antiques, hats, vinyl records, used books and some exotic candies. The owner was called Oscar Washington, and he was an excellent jeweler who sized two rings for Celeste previously. He also bought and sold used jewelry as well as designing and crafting his own.

The Velvet Sapphire didn't open until 9 AM, and it was still early. Celeste and Maybel killed some time at a quaint little coffee shop in the same strip mall. The little café served delicious chocolate croissants and espresso. If Celeste was going to play hooky from work, she needed to make it worth it, she thought, savoring the buttery flakey roll filled with warm melted chocolate. She slowly sipped her espresso that didn't have a hint of bitterness. The rain pounded the cement outside, and the two ladies sat inside chatting. A rumble of thunder rattled the café window, and a burst of lightning startled them. "This is quite a storm," Celeste said, tightening her coat around herself. She warmed her hands by holding her cup of espresso.

"I still don't understand why we are going to a jewelry shop," Maybel said, sipping her Americano coffee. She took a bit of her cinnamon dusted apple fritter.

Celeste smiled and said, "For more intel." After paying the bill, she led the way next door. They stayed under the awnings to avoid getting wet, but the rain poured down so hard in the wind it splashed everywhere.

They stepped into The Velvet Sapphire, and it gave off that faint old smell antique stores sometimes have. The bell at the top of the door rang, and Oscar appeared from behind a curtain that closed off the store from the back of the shop. He smiled sweetly at Celeste, recognizing her. "Hello honey," he greeted. The colors in his herringbone cap matched his cardigan. "My first customers of the day! How can I help you ladies?"

Celeste loved his warmth. She reached into her purse and took out the turquoise beaded hair comb showing it to him. "Will you tell me if this is real turquoise?"

"If it is not, it will be destroyed in the process. Would this upset you?" he carefully asked. Celeste shook her head no. He walked behind his front jewelry counter, pulling out a bottle of acid and a cup from a drawer behind him. He slowly poured the acid into the cup and reached out for the hair comb. He dipped the end with the turquoise beads into it and let it sit for a minute. They watched intently. Nothing happened at first. Oscar spoke, "Why don't you ladies shop around a little for a few minutes and then come back?"

They did just that. Celeste went straight to the records, flipping through them all. Maybel looked through the books. Oscar stepped up beside Celeste and told her, "I got a new Sam Cooke album in. The Rhythm and the Blues." He smiled and his worldly eyes stared into Celeste's dark eyes.

"Oh, I would love to buy that!" she responded.

"I thought you might." He was still smiling. Oscar retreated to the back to get the record for Celeste.

Poking around the store, Maybel spotted a mannequin wearing nothing but a black bra and an army helmet. She chuckled. "Oscar has a good sense of humor!" She went on, "In my day, those brassieres were so uncomfortable and pointy."

Celeste nodded. "They're still uncomfortable."

"We used to do the pencil test," Maybel said.

"The what?"

Maybel explained, "Well, this was back before women were burning their bras. Anyway, if you put a pencil under your boob, and it stayed in place, then that meant your boobs were big enough that you needed to wear a bra. George used to say a pencil could get lost under my boobs for days!"

Celeste laughed, feeling happy Maybel could enjoy her memories of her late husband.

With some items for purchase in hand, including a cookbook for Maybel that had a recipe for vegetarian chili she thought Jill would like, Maybel and Celeste strolled back to the front counter. Oscar carefully pulled the beaded hair comb out of the cup with the acid in it. When he did, they saw the bright blue turquoise beads had faded quite a bit in color to a pale blue.

"What happened?" Maybel asked.

Oscar explained, "Real turquoise is void of any carbonates, meaning it will not react to acid. Most likely this is dyed howlite–a white stone with mineral veins, similar to turquoise. Some people in the industry call it buffalo turquoise. About 90% of 'turquoise' on the market is just dyed howlite."

"So, it's not real turquoise?" Celeste asked.

"Correct," he said, wiping off the hair comb with his handkerchief.

"What does this mean?" Maybel asked Celeste.

"I'm not totally sure, but I think Jill might be selling fake turquoise and pawning it off as the real stuff, but what that has to do with Kristen's death, I do not know," Celeste answered.

Maybel took the peacock necklace out of her purse and handed it to Oscar. "Can you tell me if this is real?" she asked.

"It's real ugly," he said, chuckling. "Why did you buy this?"

"I didn't. My daughter-in-law made it for me," Maybel answered.

"Your daughter-in-law does not like you," Oscar said, looking at the necklace closely. "It's paste. There is nothing about this necklace that is real."

"How can you be sure?" Maybel inquired.

"I can do a scratch test if you want, but it may ruin the necklace," Oscar replied.

"That's fine. I'm never going to wear it again anyway," Maybel said.

Oscar took out a knife, running the edge of it along the top of one of the jade stones. The cut made a white line along the top. He took out another handkerchief and wiped the stone with it. The white line remained on the stone. He explained, "If the jade was real, the white line would wipe off. I can also tell by the color it's not real. Fake jade is usually serpentine. It's called that because it is faintly spotted, like a snake. There are some subtle brown spots on the stones." Oscar popped one of the stones out of the necklace and said, "Also, real jade is very cold to the touch and stays cold for a while. It takes a while to warm up in your hand." He handed the stone to Maybel.

"It's not cold at all!" Maybel said.

"Do you know what silver cyanide is used for?" Celeste asked.

"It's used for silver plating. A lot of jewelry is silver-plated," he answered.

"So, a jewelry maker would have it around?" Celeste asked.

"Oh, most certainly," he responded, nodding his head.

Celeste took a deep breath and felt that sick feeling in her stomach again. They thanked Oscar for his help, purchased a box of a dozen of his specialty white chocolate papaya truffles, and said goodbye, exiting the store with their merchandise.

Maybel asked, "So, what do you think we should do next, dear? I think I should talk to Jeffrey about all of this. I don't want him to be in any danger."

They put their shopping bags in Celeste's car, rain softly pelting them. The storm subsided to a drizzle.

Celeste closed her trunk, looked at Maybel in her plastic yellow rain hat, and over the sound of pitter patter rain, she asked Maybel, "Do you feel like making some vegetarian chili tonight?"

Chapter Eighteen

Afternoon Delight

That afternoon, Detective Brian Bahn went to the Jenson's manufacturing warehouse with two uniform cops, search warrant in hand, and one CSI officer. They searched it from top to bottom for silver cyanide. They found it in a back supply closet. They fingerprinted it and took it back to a lab for testing.

When he got the lab results from Kristen's left-over food and drinking glass from the wedding night, it revealed no silver cyanide found in her food or drink. He confirmed what Celeste told him about the strawberry sparkling wine bottle on the wedding table. It was the same type of strawberry liquid Kristen ingested.

Detective Bahn took Jill aside and questioned her first. Jill denied any involvement. "I don't know how Kristen drank strawberry wine!"

He calmly said to her, "Maybel said at your wedding shower, you were given a bottle of strawberry wine as a prize, and we have a video of Kristen's toast that shows the same kind of bottle on the wedding party table. If you don't know how Kristen got strawberry wine in her glass, where is your gift bottle from the shower?"

"I don't know! I can't believe you think I poisoned my best friend from childhood. She was like a sister to me! Maybel is just starting trouble because she's jealous of me for taking Jeff from her." Jill's eyes teared up.

The tears seemed real to Detective Bahn, but something was off. He asked again, "You have no recollection of what happened to your bottle of strawberry wine?"

"I got a ton of gifts that day. We loaded them up in the car, and that's all I remember," she said.

"If we search your place, will we find all the gifts from the shower, including your bottle of strawberry wine?" he asked.

"Well, you should. I certainly didn't drink that cheap stuff," Jill responded.

Detective Bahn sent the two uniform cops to her home to have it searched, and let Jill know for the time being they were done. Later, the officers told him they found no bottle of strawberry wine at Jill and Jeff's place. They did find some of her jewelry designs for the jewelry gifts Jill gave out at her wedding shower. Based on some information Celeste gave him, Detective Bahn instructed them to bring those back to the station so he could review them.

He questioned Jack Jenson after Jill. Clearly, Jack Jenson was an important man. He had the big corner office with a spectacular view overlooking the ocean. That day he wore a three-piece suit, having just come from a meeting with a potential new client. A million-dollar deal hit his taste buds, and he liked it. He needed it. He salivated over it.

Detective Bahn knew this guy's type. Jack Jenson was the kind of man that thought he was better than everyone else and that the rules didn't apply to him. He acted too busy to even be questioned by the police, so Detective Bahn pretended to be respectful and said, "I'm very sorry to bother you, sir. I know how busy you must be, and I know that time is money, but I do need to ask you a few questions."

Jack Jenson sat at his large oak executive desk, looking as annoyed as he felt. "What do you need to know?"

"Who all has access to the supply room that houses the silver cyanide?" Detective Bahn asked.

"Just a few of us–myself, the head machinist John, and his assistant… maybe one of the other jewelry makers," Jack replied.

Detective Bahn's instincts told him anymore questions would be futile to getting him the answers he needed, so he wrapped it up by asking, "Did you have lunch with your wife today?"

Jack frowned. "No, why do you ask?"

Detective Bahn motioned to his neck and said, "You've got a smudge of lipstick on your collar."

Jack Jenson turned a bright shade of pink, like the passion fruit colored smudge on his expensive dress shirt.

"Good day, sir. Thank you for your time," Detective Bahn said, smiling. He left Jack Jenson's fancy office. He then found Leah in a back corner office at a small desk. She had been scribbling some new designs on a sketch pad when he walked in.

She stood to greet him, smiling from ear to ear. "Detective Bahn, so nice to see you, especially under different circumstances. What brings you here? If you're here to talk to Jill, she just stormed out." She flipped her long hair back, rolling her eyes.

Detective Bahn was not immune to her flirting, and he ran a hand through his hair to smooth it out. He noticed her lipstick. Despite being color blind, it looked to be the same shade as what was on Jack's collar, but he couldn't be completely sure. He sat down on a chair on the opposite side of her tiny desk. "No, I'm here to see you. Did you have a nice lunch?"

Leah tilted her head to the side and wore a puzzled look on her face.

Detective Bahn went on, "Jack said you and he just got back from lunch."

"Oh, we needed to discuss some of my new designs, and we also met with a new perspective retailer who *loves* my designs. We went over a marketing plan for them. Normally Jill does the marketing, but she's a bit preoccupied right now, as you can imagine. So, as it turns out, I can successfully do design *and* sales, unlike Jill." A high-pitched titter escaped from Leah's plump lipped mouth.

"Yes, I can imagine Jill is struggling right now." Detective Bahn nodded. "I'd imagine you'd be pretty upset, too. Didn't you know Kristen really well?"

"Not as well as Jill did. Her and Kristen had been friends since childhood. I didn't meet them until we were all in college," Leah said, smiling sweetly. "I was always kind of the third wheel," she added.

"Oh, you all went to the same college?" Detective Bahn inquired.

Leah looked away and then back at him. "No, I couldn't afford to go to the same school as they did. I went to a junior college. I had to work to support myself through school too, so I worked as a server at a coffee shop. That's where I met Jill and Kristen. They came in late one night after a party and wanted pancakes. That's where it all began. They said I had the cheapest looking hair extensions they'd ever seen, and they took pity on me and wanted to befriend me." The resentment in Leah's voice echoed through the warehouse office.

"Yes, I suppose Jill and Kristen were born with silver spoons in their mouths," Detective Bahn said, chuckling. "Speaking of silver in your mouth, does it hurt to get your lip and tongue pierced?"

"I wouldn't know. I was drunk when I had mine done, along with a tattoo on my upper thigh," Leah said coyly.

Detective Bahn wondered what it was, but it seemed irrelevant to the investigation. Instead, he asked, "Weren't you with Kristen when she got her lip pierced?"

"Yeah, I suppose it was a bit uncomfortable for her. It was swollen for a few days," Leah answered.

"By the way, may I take a look at your keys to the warehouse? Jack said you have a key to the supply room," Detective Bahn asked.

"He was mistaken if he said that. I don't have a key to the supply room, but Jill does," Leah said, smiling sweetly again.

"Oh, I must have misunderstood. I'll leave you to get back to your work now. Those are really beautiful designs. Did you also design that fun peacock necklace Maybel wore to Jeff and Jill's wedding? I was thinking of getting one for my mother-in-law."

"Ugh, gawd no! That thing was hideous! That was Jill's design," Leah said, putting the word design in air quotes and snarling her upper lip. "She tried to get Jack to mass produce it, but daddy finally told her that was a no go."

"So, the peacock necklace was a one off then? Does that happen often? Handmade original pieces?" Detective Bahn inquired.

"No, not normally, but Jill usually gets whatever she wants and never has to work too hard for it," Leah replied.

A spirit of animosity floated in the air around Leah. Detective Bahn decided to play one more card. "You know, I probably shouldn't say this since Jeff and Jill just got married, but I heard a rumor that Jeff was still in love with Kristen. We probably shouldn't say anything to Jill since it would just serve to hurt her."

Leah's face froze like an iceberg, and like an iceberg, most of the ice lay beneath the surface. She spoke carefully, "I heard that rumor, too. Maybe what happened to Kristen wasn't an accident. Perhaps Jill decided to do her in, you know, to get rid of her competition." Leah tapped her pencil on her sketch pad.

"Competition? But wouldn't the competition have been over when Jeff married Jill?" Detective Bahn asked, feigning a wide-eyed innocence.

"With Jill, the competition is *never* over," Leah said.

"I suppose not." He leaned towards Leah and said in a low flirtatious voice, "That's a lovely shade of pink lipstick, and that lip ring you're wearing is really sexy. Your tongue is pierced too, isn't it?"

Leah smiled, titling her head. Her droopy eyes met his. She opened her mouth and playfully stuck out her tongue past her long teeth, revealing a silver stud piercing. She giggled and said, "Maybe sometime I can show you other things I have pierced." She held her mouth open so he could stare at her tongue piercing.

"Oh, I'd really like that," Detective Bahn said with a smoldering smile. "Celeste said Jill gave some of you jewelry she designed as gifts for helping out with the wedding. Is that the tongue ring Jill gave you?" He continued to peek at her open, inviting mouth.

Leah slid her tongue back in her mouth past her long teeth and said, "Yes. It was sweet of Jill to give us all jewelry."

"Well, I think that's all the questions I have for now. You've been very helpful." Detective Bahn stood up and exited the warehouse.

Once outside the warehouse, he looked out at the harbor. Breathing in the briny air, he listened to the seagulls squawk. The clouds from the morning rain still hovered thick in the sky, keeping the harbor dark, and hearing a ship's horn blow in the background, he thought of the puzzle pieces he'd just been handed. It was time to piece them together.

Chapter Nineteen

Shark Week

After Detective Bahn left the warehouse, he received a call from Vick. Vick informed his buddy of what transpired the night before with Leah and what her tattoo was. "It's a horseshoe! A *lucky* horseshoe!"

A little while after that, he received a call from Celeste, inviting him to dinner that night at Maybel's for some vegetarian chili. She let him in on her idea of what she wanted to do and what she suspected. He listened closely, contemplated it, and then said, "It's unorthodox, but I'm in. I'll line up a few things on my end. I'll meet you at your place a half hour before dinner so we can go over this plan again."

A couple of hours later, Maybel's crockpot of vegetarian chili bubbled, ready to go. Some sweet homemade cornbread sat in a basket on her yellow Formica table. The cornbread was an old recipe that combined a popular pancake mix and cornmeal. The cakey bread that practically melted in your mouth was another one of Jeffrey's favorite foods. Maybel invited everyone Celeste told her to, letting Jeffrey know she'd made some vegetarian chili for Jill. She also asked Jeffrey and Jill if it would be ok to look at some wedding photos that night. She thought at a time like this, the family really needed to stick together. They agreed to this. She memorized the seating order Celeste gave her and set her table for nine this time, an extra chair for Vick. Maybel intentionally gave Vick her lowest chair because she disliked him. A knock on her door indicated the line-up arrived.

The first guests to arrive were Jeffrey, Jill, Jack, and Diane, who all caravanned together since the parking at Maybel's was tricky. Maybel wanted to confide in her son, but she trusted what Celeste told her. Maybel greeted everyone, instructing them where to sit and offering beverages. A bit perturbed about having to go out in the rain, Diane asked Maybel to brew her a hot cup of tea. Maybel, ever the good hostess, prepared it quickly, asking if Diane wanted lemon or sugar with it. Diane shook her perfect but slightly wet head no. Jack asked for a scotch, Jeffrey took a beer, and Jill required a green tea, which Maybel didn't have. Jill turned her nose up at the tea Maybel offered her, saying, "I don't know who Earl Grey is."

Next to arrive were Vick and Leah, who just happened to show up to Maybel's at the same time, or so Vick let Leah think. Vick had been waiting and watching for Leah to arrive. As the president of the Home-Owners Association, he had access to the lobby security camera feed. An app on his cell phone made it possible for him to keep an eye out for her. When he spotted the lanky beauty he'd bedded the night before walking through the lobby, he rose quickly and hopped in the elevator. Both Vick and Leah accepted a beer from Maybel.

Last to arrive were Celeste and Brian, after having strategized about the evening prior to heading over to Maybel's. They had not set up a sting operation per sei, but they did come up with a good plan to get a confession from the murderer. This they knew. Because Detective Bahn was technically on duty, he requested a glass of water, and Celeste did the same.

The seating order was a bit different than it was for the engagement dinner. Celeste instructed Maybel to have her and Maybel at the head of the table, with Jill seated to Celeste's right. Jeff was next to Jill. Across from them sat Jack, Diane, and Vick. At the other end of the table sat Leah and Detective Brian Bahn.

Maybel ladled up the vegetarian chili, but Jill declined to have any, stating, "Chili is way too acidic. I can't eat it." Her little bunny nose crinkled in disgust.

Pursing her lips, Maybel offered chili to everyone else. Everyone else accepted some chili, and the basket of warm cornbread passed from person to person. Dinner was quiet and awkward, and the storm picked back up with rain pelting Maybel's north side windows.

Slipping her long foot out of her heel, Leah played footsie with Detective Bahn. She ran her big toe along the toe of his shoe, and he suppressed a laugh.

Digging into his bowl, Jeffrey said, "This chili is wonderful, mom, even though it doesn't have any meat in it."

Maybel looked over at Jill, annoyance pouring out of her eyes. "Thank you, son. Does anyone need anything else? Cheese? Onions?"

Jill snipped, "No onions, Jeff."

Detective Bahn spoke, "I'll take a dallop of that sour cream down there."

The dinner guests passed the bowl of sour cream down to him.

Celeste could feel Jill's eyes staring at her hair, and she knew she was on the right track. Earlier, Celeste fastened the fake turquoise hair comb Jill gave her on the right side of her hair, giving Jill a clear view of the beads that turned pale blue. Jill recognized this but did not say anything. Instead, Jill talked about how much she missed Kristen. "She was my best friend from elementary school." Jill sobbed. Jeffrey rested his hand on hers to comfort her. Jill dabbed at her eyes, and from behind her Kleenex, she side-eyed the telltale turquoise comb fastened to Celeste's long, dark hair.

Celeste grew tired of Jill dancing around the turquoise elephant in the middle of the room and kicked things off. "You know, Jill, the strangest thing happened. I accidentally spilled some of my nail polish remover onto the turquoise hair comb you gave me. All the turquoise beads faded to this pale blue color." Pulling the beaded comb out of her hair to hold it closer to Jill, she asked, "Do you know why that would happen?"

Jill leaned back a bit, looking uncomfortable. She said, "I'm not sure why that would happen. It's turquoise from Mexico." Jill scratched at her tiny button nose and sniffled.

"Yes, yes, you said that when you gave it to me," Celeste replied. "Leah, you know a lot about jewelry. Do you know why the nail polish remover would fade the color of the turquoise?"

Leah took her eyes off Detective Bahn and looked at Jill. Jill would not make eye contact with Leah. "Nail polish remover would never fade the color of turquoise."

"Oh, so then this isn't real turquoise?" Celeste asked, looking at Jill, feigning a puzzled look.

"We also sell costume jewelry. The stones must have gotten mixed up," Jill answered.

Celeste conversationally turned, circling in another direction and took out her cell phone. "All the photos from your wedding came out so beautiful. I know Maybel wanted to look at some pictures tonight. She hoped it would help all of us all process what happened."

"You know, Kristen asked me to take a selfie with her," Celeste said, showing Jill the picture. "It's such a nice picture of her, huh?"

Jill nodded.

"She's wearing a lip ring. I think this is the lip ring you designed for Leah, isn't it?" Celeste asked Jill, and Jill nodded again. "And at your wedding shower, Kristen didn't have a pierced lip, did she?"

Jill shook her head no, looking at Leah.

Leah averted her droopy eyes from Jill.

Everyone sat still, staying silent. Confusion clasped onto Jeffrey's face.

Celeste continued to circle. "It's the strangest thing. I checked with Detective Bahn about the lip ring Kristen was wearing at your wedding. It wasn't on her body when the coroner photographed her body and took her away. It's missing."

"It probably slipped off in all the commotion," Jack offered, setting his spoon down. He wiped some vegetarian chili from the side of his mouth.

Detective Brian Bahn joined the conversation. He turned to Leah, smiled, and said, "We saw the design for the lip ring and the tongue ring. It was genius. You did a great job designing it. We'd never seen anything like it."

"Leah didn't design it! I did!" Jill's ego strangled her throat and forced her to claim credit for the design.

Celeste moved in quick for a kill. "So, Jill, if you designed the lip ring and tongue ring, then you know the decorative round studs on them were hollow and had a tiny pinhole in each one, correct?"

"Well, they were hollow. They're cheaper to make that way," Jill said, nervously flipping her caramel-colored hair back.

Celeste bit down deeper on Jill with an accusation. "The hollow round studs could also be removed, filled with poison, and put back on. The rings were placed in jewelry boxes with the pinholes facing up, so nothing would leak out. Then, when someone put on the lip ring or tongue ring, the poison would leak out of the pinhole and into their mouth…"

"I don't know anything about a pinhole!" Jill shouted.

Jeffrey sat quietly next to her, frowning at Celeste. Thinking about what Celeste implied, he felt his heart sink to the bottom of the ocean, and it hurt.

"I think you do know something about it, and I think you intentionally poisoned Kristen because you were jealous of her. You knew Jeff loved her," Celeste said.

A protesting slip escaped Jill's mouth, "I didn't try to kill Kristen! I tried to kill Leah because of the blackmail."

She cracked easily, Celeste thought. She looked at Jack. He sat silent and didn't move. Celeste, not quite done, bit Jill again with another accusation. "Your dad put you on a budget and wouldn't pay off your credit card debt. You were getting desperate. You were selling your fake turquoise and fake jade as real to make more money on the side, and Leah knew about this. She was blackmailing you, correct? And if news about the fake turquoise and jade selling as the real stuff got out, it would ruin your dad's company's reputation."

Jill nodded, which confirmed what Detective Bahn had already dug up. Jack Jenson made some recent deals that went south. His balance sheet took quite a hit in the past couple of years.

Jeffrey turned to his wife and asked, "Jill, how could you do this to us?"

"Jeff, I really do love you! I did this for us. Don't you see? Leah could have ruined everything!" Jill screeched.

Leah threw that hot potato accusation off her as fast as she could. "I didn't blackmail anyone! This is absurd!"

Celeste spoke to Leah, "Vick told us the night of the wedding he drove you home, and you asked him to stop off at the warehouse. He said you took home a blue folder of turquoise and jade payables and receivables. Why would you do this?"

"You have no proof of that." Defiantly, Leah stuck her nose in the air.

Vick reached for Leah's hand and said, "Sorry babe but I took some photos of what was in that folder after we made love on your smooth satin sheets…" He whispered to her, "That was *outstanding,* by the way."

Leah snorted, pulled her hand away from him, and shouted, "I'm not your babe! You hairy ape!"

Triumphantly, Maybel smiled.

"Leah, the proof of what Jill was doing, and your blackmail of it was in that folder, along with the howlite and serpentine receipts. We have photos of it," Celeste continued, "also, I'm sure your company's purchases and sales are all done online. It would be easy enough to obtain."

Leah protested again, "So what? All I did was call Jill out on her fraud. You have no proof of me blackmailing her. She thought she could design better than me! What a joke! Even John showed me her designs to see if I could help fix them. Her jewelry was crap, and she knew it! Jack knows it! He knows I design better than her. It was bad enough she took Jeff from me, but she wasn't going to take my career too! I did nothing wrong."

"I think you did." Celeste circled around for another kill with more accusations. "I think you intentionally switched jewelry with Kristen."

Leah spoke quickly and loudly, "I didn't want to wear that ugly lip ring Jill made, and it didn't fit my lip, and Kristen liked it, so we switched. Big deal. I didn't know it was poison. Jill doesn't even love Jeff! She just loved taking him away from me! And don't even get me started on Kristen. Jill knew Jeff still carried a torch for her. That's probably why she tried to kill her!"

Celeste bit down hard on Leah, ripping her flesh with her theory. She said, "I think you did know it was a poisonous lip ring. You stated it didn't fit, but you would have had to try it on to know it didn't fit. But if you had tried it on, you would have gotten poison in your mouth. You would have gotten very sick, maybe even died.

"Also, the day of my open house, you told me you had seen all of Jill's designs. We've seen her designs, too. And since you saw her designs, you saw what we saw. You also said John showed you Jill's designs to see if you could fix them. That's when you saw the holes in the silver round studs. At first, you probably assumed that due to a lack of experience, Jill put a hole in the wrong spot, but when John told you Jack asked him to set the design by filling the hollow ring and round stud with silver cyanide, you knew there was only one reason for that. You figured it out and switched jewelry with Kristen, trying to make it look like Jill killed Kristen. At the warehouse, you told Detective Bahn you were wearing the tongue ring Jill gave you, but that was a lie. I think if Detective Bahn searches your place, he'll find the poison tongue ring completely untouched. You knew not to wear it."

Blood flowed out into the water now...

Leah wished to God someone would throw her a life preserver. Through wilted, teary eyes, she looked at Detective Bahn, hoping it would be him. She knew he liked her. Maybe he'd go easy on her. She uttered to him, "I want a lawyer."

"Sure," Detective Bahn said. "But there is another item Celeste wants to discuss with Jack, right Celeste?"

"Right," Celeste said, circling again, ready to create a frenzy of accusations in the water. "Jack, you knew Leah tried to blackmail Jill, didn't you? Jill told you what Leah was trying to do to her, and to your company. You put the pinhole in the silver round studs. You filled them with silver cyanide. It was really your idea, wasn't it? You sign off on all the manufacturing of the designs, and I think you modified the design for the lip ring and tongue ring.

"Wait, correction. You probably didn't want to get your hands dirty, so you had one of your machinists put the pinholes in the silver round studs and fill them with silver cyanide and he did this for you, too. Because of a thing called plausible deniability, he didn't know why the designs were like this. Or you just told him the silver cyanide would help set the designs and that you'd remove it later, but you didn't remove it, did you?"

Jack had been sitting frozen since Celeste pulled the comb out of her hair. He finally moved, wiping his mouth again with his napkin held in trembling hands, the taste of honey butter from the cornbread still on his lips. He too requested a lawyer. "I'm going to get a cease-and-desist order! You can't make accusations like this against me! I won't have it out there!"

Jack's threat dripped off Celeste, making no impact on her. She said, "Yes, you will need a lawyer if my original theory is correct. However, that lawyer may need to represent someone else along with you and your daughter. I thought about it some more, and I remembered that old rule about poison usually being a woman's weapon. Something still doesn't add up, especially since the amount of silver cyanide in only the lip ring wasn't enough to kill someone, just make them really sick. Yet Kristen died from it."

Jack bellowed, "I've had enough of these accusations! What an embarrassment to this family evening!"

Celeste went on, "Someone brought the bottle of sparkling strawberry wine on board and made sure Kristen drank it. You and your daughter were only trying to kill Leah. You four all knew Kristen had a severe allergy to strawberries. Jack, this isn't looking good for you. Brian and I saw you hand Kristen the glass of strawberry wine for her toast and when she had an allergic reaction, none of you even tried to get her EpiPen."

Jill sobbed, hiding her face with her hands.

Leah crossed her skinny arms across her chest and slipped her slinky foot back into her heel.

Jack sat frozen.

Diane burst under the pressure of the bite. "Jack didn't do it! I did!"

Jack's deep voice commanded, "Diane, shut up!"

Diane took a deep breath and said, "It doesn't matter. We're screwed! They have all the evidence they need. To save money, we brought some gift bottles of wine onboard with us for the toast. When we were below deck, I spoke to Jill right before the ceremony started. She was in a panic. She told me what she and her father had done, and how Kristen ended up with the lip ring. I saw the strawberry wine. I improvised and made sure Jack gave Kristen a glass of it for the toast. He didn't even know what kind of wine it was. Neither did Jill. I wanted to make it look like an allergic reaction, so no one would know about the poisonous lip ring."

This was a case of 'like Mother, like daughter' with the strawberry wine being as deadly to Kristen as poison would have been to Leah. Celeste had one last biting accusation. "Jill," she said, turning to look at her, "When you were crying and screaming over Kristen, you pulled the lip ring off Kristen's lip, didn't you?"

Jack shouted, "Jill, don't answer any more questions!"

"She doesn't have to answer. We respect your right to seek legal counsel. You're going to need it. But I just want to point out that if you did pull the lip ring off her, that is probably what caused traces of the silver cyanide poison to get on the outside of Kristen's mouth. That poison then got in Detective Brian Bahn's mouth when he performed CPR on her. I'm not sure if you can be charged for the attempted murder of Detective Bahn, but I think at a minimum, it's reckless endangerment.

I'll have to defer to Detective Bahn and the lawyers on that," Celeste said.

Detective Bahn nodded, adding, "And tampering with evidence."

Silence sunk into the room like a treasure chest full of jewels hitting the bottom of the ocean floor.

Jill, Leah, Jack, and Diane all bled out from the shark attack.

Maybel, ever the delightful hostess, asked, "So, who wants dessert?"

Chapter Twenty

Turning the Tables

Four uniform police officers waited outside Maybel's condo. At Detective Bahn's instruction, they handcuffed and took Jill, Leah, Diane, and Jack into custody.

A pained look fell on Maybel's face, and she explained, "Jeffrey, I'm sorry I didn't tell you what we planned for tonight, but Celeste advised me against it."

Jeffrey sat, stunned at his mom's yellow Formica table, the table he'd sat at so many times before the table he grew up doing his homework on and learning lessons. But this lesson was the hardest one of all. "It's OK. If you had told me what you suspected, I wouldn't have believed you. I needed to hear the confession with my own ears," he said, looking sullen. "I can't believe I married a murderer. I'm a simple man, and I just wanted a simple woman."

"Well, did you consummate your marriage? If you didn't, maybe you could get an annulment," Maybel said.

"I knew something was off about her, but she was so sweet at first," Jeffrey reasoned. "There were some warning signs, like her temper tantrums. They were crazy. Also, the night I asked her to marry me and gave her the ring, she kept posting on social media and wouldn't even enjoy the candlelight dinner I cooked for us. I just wanted to be alone with her and enjoy the moment, but she wouldn't stop looking at her phone. And she wasn't really a vegan either, not that it matters, but I know she ate chicken and burgers because I found fast food wrappers in the back seat of her car."

Maybel bristled and asked, "You mean to tell me that bitch ate meat!? What am I going to do with all this vegetarian chili she wouldn't eat?! I don't even think you can call it chili if it doesn't have meat in it. Do they serve vegan food in prison?"

Vick shook his head. "I can't believe I slept with a murderer, too, but she was like a kinky little mare. She rode my—"

"OK," Celeste interrupted, "I think we should leave and give Maybel and Jeffrey some privacy. I'm sure they have a lot to talk about."

Brian and Vick followed her out. When they approached Celeste's door, Vick asked, "Do you think Jeff has some sort of magic down there? I mean, why were all these hot chicks fighting over him? What's he got going on?"

Celeste thought Vick's question was gross. She shook her head. "I don't think any of this was even about Jeff so much as it was about Jill and Leah's competitiveness with each other. I mean, they treated Jeff like a prize and not a human being. If Jill actually cared about Jeff, she wouldn't have done something so horrible. Now her marriage is ruined by it before it even had a chance to blossom."

"And don't forget greed," Brian added, "Jill's greed to make more money off the fake jewelry and Leah's greed to take it from her. What a tangled web they wove. You know that thing they say about money being the root of all evil."

Celeste clarified, "I hate to nitpick, but the saying is actually 'the love of money is the root of all evil'. Money in it of itself is not evil, but the *love* of money over other things leads to all kinds of evil."

Vick interjected, "Well, if those chicks wanted to use me as a prize, I'd be the game all night long."

Celeste frowned. "Vick, they're murderers."

Vick contemplated this and said, "I'm not saying I want to marry Leah or anything like that, but maybe a visit once in a while when she gets lonely. How hot would a conjugal visit be?"

Celeste shook her head at Brian, and Brian said to Vick, "Hey buddy, conjugal visits are for spouses only. Why don't you go back to your place, and I'll text you later, OK? Great work with all of this! I really appreciate it."

Vick smiled proudly from ear to ear and said good-bye to them. He headed to the elevator while Brian walked Celeste back to her place. "That was some great work too, Ms. Ravenna. I couldn't have cracked them better myself," he complimented her. "We recorded it all. Leah also confessed to Vick last night during a pillow talk session. She admitted she knew Jill designed a poison lip ring and tongue ring and was trying to kill her. She told Vick she thought when Jill saw Kristen with the lip ring on, she'd be a decent human being and make Jill take the lip ring off. She said she still had the tongue ring, too. We sent officers over to her place tonight, and they found it, so that will really lock all this down, just like you said." Brian held up his phone to show the text he'd received with the information.

"What? You mean you already had a witness Leah confessed to? Why did you let me do this tonight?" Celeste wondered, feeling angry.

"I wanted to watch you operate, and we didn't have a confession from anyone else. Instinct told me you'd be able to get it," Brian said, his face filling with deep creases from his arrogant grin. "We make a good team. Are you looking for a job? You could work for me."

"No. I have a good job, and I have to start packing up my place. I'm moving to my new townhouse soon."

"I suppose I'll get an invitation over for dinner," he said, still smiling.

"Only if you're bringing it. I'm not cooking for you just because you tell me to. I'll only do it if I want to." Celeste's defiant tone amused Brian.

"So feisty!" Brian said. "Well, I've got to go. I have to get back to the station. I've got a lot of paperwork to do on this one, but I just have one question for *you*, Celeste. How did you know the lip and tongue rings had poison in them?"

"You said in the designs you saw that the loops and round studs on them were hollow," Celeste answered.

"I think you knew they held poison in them before I told you the design details. That's why you asked about the design details in the first place," Brian said, and in his mind's eye, he saw a gypsy turning over a tarot card.

"On instinct I suspected Kristen's death had something to do with the lip ring, and then when you told me the design details with the pinholes, I added that together with the silver cyanide found in Kristen's body, and then I knew for sure what they had done. How did you know I knew before you told me about the designs?" Celeste asked.

Brian smiled and answered, "I didn't, but I do now because I just used one of your confession techniques on you."

Celeste gasped and screeched, "You can't out technique me!" Her competitive streak standing straight on end.

"Uh, yeah, I just did!" Brian snorted. "And now I've disarmed you, and you won't be able to use that technique on me." His grin kissing his ears, he felt pleased with himself.

Celeste's brow was so furrowed she could have knit a scarf with it. "That's not my only technique!"

"I'm sure I'll figure out your other techniques," he said. He paused and whispered, "and when I do, I'm going to use those on you, too." He winked at her.

Celeste was no longer knitting a scarf. Now it was a blanket!

He reached out and messed up her hair. Celeste couldn't duck in time but swatted his hand away. "Let me know when you want me to bring dinner over to your new place," Brian said confidently, still grinning a grin that put lines in his cheeks.

Celeste went inside and shut her door, feeling mad but laughing and shaking her head. Emotionally, it felt like a shark lurked on the other side of the door, but was she a shark, too? Could one shark be afraid of another shark? Those were questions she'd have to answer another time. But for that night, she lived to swim another day…

Chapter Twenty-One

Accessories to Murder

A little while after Maybel and Jeffrey had a heart to heart talk, Maybel went next door to Celeste's. She huffed, "Jeffrey won't tell me if he consummated his marriage. He told me not to worry about it." She plopped down on Celeste's white couch, relaying her conversation with him. "Can you believe tonight!? A quadruple murder!"

"I think it's quadruple murderers." Celeste sat down next to her.

"Oh yeah, that's right. Talk about *accessories* to murder!" Maybel mused.

"Brian said Leah confessed to Vick last night."

"That A-hole withheld evidence from us?!" Maybel asked.

"Well, we're not the police, so Vick wasn't obligated to tell us."

"By the way, dear, can we go over what happened to Kristen? I'm not sure I followed everything that just went down," Maybel asked.

Celeste explained, "Jill was pawning off fake turquoise and fake jade as the genuine stuff to make extra money. Leah found out and started blackmailing her because she wanted in on the cash. Leah threatened to expose what Jill was doing, which could have ruined Jill's dad's company. Jill went to her dad and told him about Leah's blackmail. They came up with the poison lip and tongue ring plan and probably figured when they killed Leah, they could claim it was an accident and claim it was because the machinist didn't remove the silver cyanide from the hollow rings and round studs on the lip and tongue rings. But then Leah saw Jill's designs with the pinholes in the round studs and figured out what Jill was trying to do to her when John Swormy mentioned to Leah that Jack asked him to put some silver cyanide inside the rings and studs to set the design.

"Then Leah switched jewelry with Kristen, which would make Leah the murderer since she knew the lip ring had poison in it. But if no one could prove Leah knew the lip ring and tongue ring had poison in them, then it would be blamed on only Jill. Leah was supposed to wear the jewelry to the wedding, but when Jill saw that Kristen was wearing the poisonous lip ring, she panicked. She told her mom, and then her mom Diane, wanting to protect her family and the family business, came up with the plan to give Kristen some of the strawberry wine to cover up the poison lip ring murder attempt. Since Diane knew what a severe allergy Kristen had to strawberries, Diane figured she could make it look like Kristen died of anaphylactic shock instead, and no one would suspect a poison lip ring."

"Oh, that poor Kristen didn't stand a chance. God rest her soul," Maybel said, shaking her head. "But wouldn't she have tasted the silver cyanide in the lip ring?"

"No," Celeste said, "Kristen mentioned that her and Leah did Jägermeister shots right before they got on the boat. Leah probably gave the lip ring to Kristen to wear and then had them do shots to cover up the taste of it."

"So, all four of them tried to kill Kristen?"

"No, only Leah and Diane directly tried to kill Kristen. Jill and Jack were trying to kill Leah."

"Kristen just got caught in the crossfire of all of this, and it was Kristen's poisonous lips that made Brian sick, right?"

"Yes, but the real poisonous lips were from the toxic words Leah spoke, creating such hatred between her and Jill," Celeste answered. "But the question I still have is why would one bridesmaid want to kill another bridesmaid?"

"Dear, I think I can answer that. After you all left, Jeffrey and I had a good heart to heart conversation. He told me he did still have feelings for Kristen, but a while back, Kristen made it clear to him it was over between them. They still kept in touch and texted from time to time. Strictly platonic, but Jeff maintained a friendship with her. Well, he was just telling me that Jill found out about the texts and went crazy on him. Jill also let Leah know Jeff and Kristen were still communicating on a regular basis.

"I think Leah thought if she switched the poison lip ring and took Kristen out and it got blamed on Jill, she'd knock out two birds with one stone. Jeff said he knew Leah still carried a torch for him and tried to get back together with him all the time. And do you know that Leah met Jeffrey first? Even before he met Kristen, Leah was carrying a torch for him. In a way, I think Leah loved Jeffrey the most, and she loved him first."

Celeste added, "Like I was saying to Vick and Brian, I think all of this was more about Jill and Leah's competitiveness, their egos, and their greed and not about Jeff at all. They treated him like a trophy and not a person, and they both resented each other so much."

"Oh, and what about Jack and Diane?" Maybel asked.

"The family business is their empire, and the thing that afforded them such a lavish lifestyle over the years. You'd be surprised how far people will go to protect what's theirs, what they spent so many years sacrificing to build," Celeste said.

Maybel shook her head. "For the first time since George passed, I'm glad he wasn't here. I would have hated for him to see this atrocious behavior. And poor Jeffrey had no idea what he was getting into. Do you think all four of them will be charged with murder?" Maybel wondered.

"Probably, or at least attempted murder, or conspiracy to commit murder, or something like that. It will be for the lawyers to figure out."

"You know, to be honest with you, I think Jeffrey is relieved he's off the hook with Jill. He said he'd been having so many doubts about her, but he thought that was just normal."

"I'm the last person that can weigh in on what's normal in relationships. I just got angry because Brian figured out one of the techniques I use on insurance claimants and then he used it on me!" Celeste laughed at herself.

"Dear, where do you think things are going with you and Brian?" Maybel wondered.

"I'm not sure. I mean, sometimes he's just so sexist and arrogant, but when I saw him jump into action at the wedding, take charge of everything and risk his own life to help someone. It's hard to put into words, but I'm glad I got to see that side of him. And the day I took him your chicken noodle soup, I saw a couple of things that softened my opinion of him. Plus, I really appreciate the fact that he respected me enough to listen to my plan about how to get everyone to confess tonight," Celeste answered.

Maybel smiled and said, "Dear, I know I'm from a different generation, but I'd like to think I'm pretty open-minded. I'd like to give you some advice. No man is perfect. You find the one that speaks to your heart, and out of love, you forgive all the things they do. That's just how it is. How many times do we as women label men as neanderthals, and isn't that reverse sexism on our part? Maybe we don't always appreciate what they try to do for us. Brian is very masculine, and in time, I think you will learn to accept that for what it is. It's difficult for you now because you're so independent, but if you let your guard down a little, I think he has a lot he could offer to you."

Celeste contemplated this motherly advice, and she knew it came from a place of love.

Maybel shifted gears, saying, "I told Jeff he needs to talk to me more about his life. If he'd just let me know what all was really going on, I could have helped him. He agreed to do that, but on only one condition."

"That you stop asking him if he consummated his marriage?" Celeste asked.

"No, he wants me to move to that retirement home, Shady Sunset." Maybel looked down at her hands.

"How do you feel about that?" Celeste wondered.

"Well, it's still in Sunshine Beach, but it's closer to his work. It will be easier for him to visit more," she said. "Also, I have a few friends there. You know, my friend Vera lives there. She says the place is great. They have activities for the residents, and everyone is really social over there. Jeffrey doesn't think this building is safe for me anymore, considering everything that happened last year."

Celeste gave Maybel a hug. "You are going to be so happy there. It's in the stars. I think it's just what you need. We can face chat now that you have a new phone, and you can order a car ride over to my place for Saturday lunches. This is going to be good for both of us." Celeste smiled.

"Vera said there's a bit of a singles scene there. Who knows, I may meet someone." Maybel gave a shrug. "I think a change will do me good."

"A change will do both of us good! We'll have to help each other pack," Celeste suggested. "Do you have any more of those blondies?"

Both ladies giggled, and in the weeks to follow, they had the best packing parties ever.

Chapter Twenty-Two

The Rhythm and the Blues

Celeste closed the escrow on both places, and she settled into her new townhouse. The movers placed everything where she instructed them to, and with her friend Veronica's help, they got most of her boxes unpacked. It took Celeste a few nights, but she finally got used to all the unfamiliar noises at her place.

She purchased some colorful artwork and hung paintings all over the walls. Her east wall was covered in brick, and she didn't hang anything on that wall. The brick was so beautiful on its own. It felt like a terracotta paradise. She set up a cozy reading nook under her staircase with a plush, tufted chaise lounge, a Tiffany-style reading lamp, and a walnut bookcase full of her favorite books and knick-knacks. She placed various green leafy plants in sunny corners of her home. She fastened a bird swing from her raised ceiling for Birino, and he loved it, often walking along the railing that lined her second-floor loft. She gave away her old couch to Goodwill and bought a new plush emerald green one with storage under one cushion. Since her place was small, she needed to be smart about how she used the space.

For the outside, she decided on some dark rattan patio furniture with rusty orange cushions and hung some twinkle lights from the patio cover. Happy to embark on a new beginning, she felt quite accomplished. Just as she moved her residence to a new place, she decided to move her relationship with Brian to a new place.

Her second weekend in the townhouse, per Dr. Fisher's homework assignment, she decided to act out of love and not fear. She invited Brian over for dinner. She stood at her second story rear window looking down at the street and watched him get out of his convertible with a takeout bag in his hand. She hurried down the stairs to greet him.

He brought Japanese food. He acted nonchalant about it, but the truth was when she called, he came running. Unbeknown to her, he'd even manscaped before their date. "I still can't believe how you took down all four of them so quickly," Brain said, popping a dumpling with plum sauce in his mouth. He also brought along with him an expensive bottle of aged Sake. He clinked his glass to Celeste's and downed it. It warmed him from the inside.

Sitting side by side with him at her bar and shrimp tempura in front of them, Celeste smiled and said, "They were caught off guard because I was asking the questions and not you. A sneak attack." Celeste sipped her cold Sake, and it burned her throat. When Brian offered her more, she shook her head. "One is my limit." She knew what might happen if she had more than one.

Brian poured himself a second shot glass full of the stuff that gave him courage.

"I take it you got all your paperwork for the case done?"

"Yeah, that was no small task. We've gone through enough of their financial records now to know Jill was pocketing at least an extra $1,000 a week from her fake turquoise and jade scam. We think she switched out the genuine stuff for the fake stuff she bought, and John Swormy didn't know and used the stones in what they were manufacturing. Then Jill sold the genuine stuff on the side, pocketing the cash."

"No wonder Leah wanted in on it. Maybel had a theory about why Leah switched the poison jewelry with Kristen. She thought she could 'kill two birds with one stone' as they say and take out both Kristen and Jill and then have Jeff to herself. But it's still a bit puzzling to me. I get why Leah would turn on Jill and want to get Jill in trouble because Jill was trying to kill Leah, but I can't believe Leah would intentionally give the poison lip ring to Kristen, knowing it would harm her. I guess that's how deep-seated Leah's resentment of Jill and Kristen was. I think she felt that Jill and Kristen thought they were better than her because they came from money."

"Yeah, it's just a whole other level of crazy. When I first met Leah, I thought she was crazy for Jeff, like singing *You're So Vain* by Carly Simon at a karaoke bar kind of crazy. But she's more like *Fatal Attraction* kind of insanity. But what I can't believe is that Maybel kept quiet about everything and didn't spill the beans to Jeff about what we were going to do at dinner. I wonder how Jeff is dealing with all of this now."

"Maybel said he seems to be doing OK. I think all of this strengthened their relationship. He's been spending more time with her lately. He's even planning an 80th birthday celebration for her. He wants us all to go to an amusement park for it. He said she hasn't been in years," Celeste replied.

Brian smiled. "I love churros. I'm in!"

"I wanted to ask you a couple of questions," Celeste began, and Brian nodded. "Why did you get divorced twice?"

Brian put down his chopsticks and looked at her, the question stirring up old memories in him. He knew he couldn't lie to her, but not because he wasn't capable of that, but because she would know if he did. "My first wife, Denise, was never happy. I tried. I swear. I think she had really high expectations of what marriage would be like and always felt disappointed. I worked long hours, and she felt neglected. Nothing I did was ever good enough. She didn't want to have kids either, so I got a vasectomy for her. The irony is she left me and ended up marrying a doctor who works longer hours than I do, and they have two kids now.

"My second wife, Tonya, I will admit I married on a rebound. I also neglected to tell her before we got married that I had the vasectomy. When she found out, she felt betrayed, accused me of lying to her, and never could really forgive me for it, but in my defense, we never actually talked about having kids, so technically, I didn't lie to her."

"She probably thought it was a lie by omission. Couldn't you just have had it reversed?" Celeste wondered.

"I guess, but the truth is, I didn't want to snip it back for her. I didn't really want to have kids with her." He looked down at his plate. "She basically put a noose around the relationship and just kept pulling on it as hard as she could. I'm still paying for it… literally. The alimony is killing me. She's even got some new guy that wants to get married, but I think she's holding off just so she can make me pay for what she thinks I did to her."

Celeste looked at him for a few moments and knew this was the truth. She appreciated that he told it to her, and after a pause, she said, "I think there is something else you want to tell me."

Brian quietly said, "I never really loved her, and I was unfaithful to her. I also never want to get married again."

Why would he? Celeste wondered.

He went on, "I think too many people place too much importance on monogamy. Humans aren't meant to be monogamous. We're meant to be wild and free. So, what about you? You ever been married?"

"No. I was engaged once to a slick insurance salesman who could talk anyone into anything, including me. I finally came to my senses when I caught him cheating on me," Celeste answered.

"So, you have trust issues?" Brian asked.

"Does that really matter?" Celeste got up and took her plate to the sink.

"Was that your only significant relationship?" he wondered.

"No, there was another one, a cop, very alpha male and very controlling. Everyone else was just casual dating," she explained.

He laughed. "I can't imagine you being controlled by anyone. Did you love him?"

Old memories got a hold of her, practically strangling her throat. "Why would you ask me that?"

"Celeste, that's not an answer." Brian looked at her.

"I cared for both of them, but in hindsight, I don't think I was really in love with either of them. I don't think I've ever been in love. I must be broken."

"We're all broken, kid. Some of us are just better at hiding it than others." Brian leaned his arm up against hers.

"What is love, anyway? People think it's just a bunch of warm fuzzy feelings and raging hormones that make you do crazy things, but that's not what it is. Love is something you *do*, not something you *feel*. Love is being kind and caring and forgiving."

Brian nudged her with his arm again and said, "Sounds like you know more about love than you think you do."

Perched on her barstool, Celeste asked, "Is this when we start having a serious conversation about why we're here on earth and the meaning of life?"

"Nah," he replied, "I was going to ask you if you like jazz?"

With a giggle, Celeste said, "No. What's your sign?"

"I'm a Leo," Brian replied, reaching for another dumpling. "What's yours?"

"I'm a cancer."

"Which one is that? The fish?"

Celeste shook her head. "No, it's the crab."

"That fits you!"

Celeste frowned. "How so?"

"I feel like we just keep moving sideways and not forward, like a crab moves along the beach."

Celeste laughed. "Well, at least we're moving. Oh! Speaking of the beach, did you see the magazine issue Jill, Leah, and Kristen were in?"

The shake of Brian's head prompted Celeste to get out her copy of Bridal Wave magazine. There was an angry-looking picture of Jill on the cover with the headline 'California Cutie Charged with Murder'.

"Well, Jill wanted to be famous, so she got her ten minutes of fame," Brain said, reading the article.

A second shot of pear Sake warmed Celeste's throat as she threw it back.

"Are these cookie bars?" he asked, seeing a plate of Maybel's blondies on the bar.

"No, no. Those aren't for tonight." Celeste quickly moved them away. "I made something else for your dessert."

Brian raised his eyebrows. "So, you did cook?"

"Barely." With a carton in her hand from the freezer, she put his dessert together.

He dug into his sundae. "What are these little pink crunchy things? They're so good."

"Raspberry sprinkles."

He took another bite of his coconut ice cream, topped with her sugar-coated gift to him. "I thought you said you made those up." He crunched another one, and it burst with sweet and sour raspberry.

"I thought I did, but then I came up with a recipe for them. I candied some freeze-dried raspberries and chopped them up after they hardened. I felt guilty for making fun of you for your elaborate beverage choices, and I'm trying to make up for that," she said, smiling sweetly.

"Why, Miss Ravenna, I do believe you have a crush on me." He took another bite of his coconut ice cream, licking his spoon, looking glib and wanting to gloat all over her.

Shifting gears, she asked, "There's another question I've been meaning to ask you. Do you read the newspaper every day?"

"No, I don't read the newspaper. Why do you ask?"

"When I was at your place, I saw a stack of newspapers. They were next to a can of red spray paint," she said.

"I couldn't find a candy apple red baton, so I bought a silver one and spray painted it red for you. That's what the newspapers were for. I set the baton on the newspapers when I spray painted it."

"I have another question for you, if you don't mind." She paused and looked at him, feeling his knee touching hers. He nodded, and she went on, "Your tattoo. How long have you had it?"

He set his spoon down, and she spotted a flash of embarrassment hit his face. Carefully, she said, "I think you first had the tattoo of the heart hanging from the noose. My guess is, after hearing what you said tonight about your second wife, you probably got the heart noose tattoo when you were with your second wife. But recently, you added a raven holding the noose in its mouth with the dangling heart."

He nodded.

She asked, "Are you grieving the loss of your lady love like in the poem *The Raven* by Edgar Allan Poe?"

A few quiet seconds sat between them. "This '*Tell-Tale Heart*' of mine gives me away, huh?" He stared back at her. He reached out and twirled a lock of her hair around his fingers and whispered, "Maybe the tattoo is for your raven-colored hair…"

A pregnant pause filled the air. Fate brought this man to her, and she wanted to move forward but wasn't sure how. Shifting gears, she said, "I used another one of my confession techniques on you. I had no idea if you really had something else to tell me. It was just an instinct, so I pushed, and confidence is half the bluff. But confession is good for the soul." Celeste smiled. He told her the truth that night, and for the first time, she trusted him. She willingly set her weapons down and hoped she'd never have to pick them up again. Wisdom told her she wouldn't be able to change Brian. She would need to accept him as he was, flaws and all, and in doing so, perhaps he'd accept her, flaws and all. Could it be that easy? No way.

Brian got up and looked around closely at the first floor of Celeste's new home. "Man, this place is so cool! I love all the paintings and pictures you have on the walls. This place feels like an art gallery," he astutely observed. He looked at a stack of vinyl records sitting on the ground by Celeste's new antique record cabinet. While flipping through them, Celeste let him know some of them were Maybel's.

For a house-warming gift, Maybel gave Celeste her record collection. Maybel moved to Shady Sunset Retirement Home and lived in a smaller place than at Regal Palms. She told Celeste she didn't think she'd have room for them, but really, she just wanted Celeste to have them. "Here, let's play this one. I got it at The Velvet Sapphire the day everyone was arrested. I never got the chance to listen to it," Celeste said, handing Brian the Sam Cooke album.

He placed it on the turntable, and the needle cracked and popped when it hit the vinyl. With soulful music playing, he helped her unpack her records away in the cabinet. Once that was done, a little help from the Sake gave him the nerve to ask her to dance. He held out his hand to her, and she took it. Behind broken hearted lyrics, piano keys were tickled, and a saxophone bellowed low and slow. Bodies close, Brian rested his hands on her hips, taking the lead, moving his feet to the rhythm.

Celeste reached up and put her hands on his shoulders, high school prom style, and she wondered if he was as good at everything he does as he was at dancing. With heads tilted to opposite sides, Celeste smiled and asked herself why had she been fighting it? High above them, Birino perched on his bird swing, his bird cage squeaking.

They swayed to the music slowly at first with the Brazilian hardwood floor under foot. Celeste followed Brian's lead. His rhythm chased away her blues, and her flamenco red dress flared out as they twirled around. Brian, always light on his feet, dipped her unexpectedly, and Celeste's heart jumped at the surprise. With one leg up in the air, she wondered if he'd drop her, but he pulled her back up, holding her tight to him. He coaxed her body to move the way he wanted it to. He spun her around, and their date was giving all the Saturday night vibes.

The song changed, and a more upbeat tempo rang out from the record player. The entire horn section blasted out the tune. When the next song sang out '*Twisting the Night Away*', he did a bit of a torso swivel, and Celeste followed his lead again, twisting her hourglass figure around him. With the sands of time pouring out before them, they moved in tandem, synchronizing arms in and arms out. Feet shuffled back and forth, faster than a deck of cards dealing someone's luck. Their bodies flowed close to each other, then ebbed away from each other, then back again. She laughed at the tickle on her neck, and her long hair flipped about, brushing across his face when he strutted behind her.

The next song sang out softly from the record player, slow and sappy. Face to face again, Brian looked into her dark eyes that burned hotter than coal and sparkled brighter than diamonds. Gazing at her felt like looking at a vintage lingerie ad. The innocence of her nostalgic look made him feel warm and fuzzier than a peach.

He'd seen so much death in his career that his own mortality stared back at him. Knowing time is a precious gift, he whispered in Celeste's ear, "I could dance with you forever."

Like the water floods the ocean shore in a tidal wave, a blush flooded Celeste's face. "Forever is a long time, Detective Bahn."

His eyes looked like shooting stars. "It sure is, Miss Ravenna." Brian knew Celeste's iceberg heart was melting down to an ice cube. It was just a matter of time…

The tide of the dance washed over them, and Celeste surfed around with Brian to the music. He pulled her close again, keeping his hands on her. She wasn't sure she agreed with his views on relationships and sex, but that night, she knew she wanted to keep dancing.

And Brian's timing really was *impeccable*…

Raspberry Sprinkles Recipe

Ingredients:
½ cup freeze-dried raspberries
1 tablespoon butter (NOT a heaping tablespoon)
1 tablespoon sugar

Prep and cook time: 5 minutes

Heat butter up in a tiny skillet. Add in sugar and mix up quickly, throwing in the raspberries as soon as that is done. Keep the heat on the stove low, as they can burn easily. Mix around the raspberries constantly in the butter and sugar mixture for a few minutes. (Again, don't do this too long, or they will burn.)

Take them out of the skillet and set them on a plate to dry and harden. Approximately an hour.

Once they've dried and hardened, you can chop them up with a knife, breaking them up into smaller pieces.

You can use the raspberry sprinkles to put on ice cream, cupcakes, cookies, yogurt, donuts, or whatever you like. They're your sprinkles to do what you want with.

Enjoy!

If you want to find out what's next for Celeste, Brian, Maybel, and Vick, look for a book coming soon called:

The Crying Place

About the Author

Drew Dunmoore is a California native and enjoys visiting local amusement parks. Drew has worked in the financial services industry for twenty years but has been obsessed with murder mysteries for more than thirty years. This is Drew's second book, and God willing, there will be many more to come.

To find out more about the Celeste Ravenna Mystery Series, or to contact Drew, check out the following:

Follow Drew on Instagram: @drewdunmoore

www.dunmooredisports.com

Readers can reach Drew at ddunmoore@gmail.com